SINK HMS COSSACK

In this action-packed, fictionalised account of the most famous destroyer in World War II, the doyen of naval fiction re-tells the story through the eyes of Wide Boy, a Cockney spiv who starts out cynically, but eventually sacrifices himself to save others when the ship is finally sunk in 1941.

Recent Titles by Duncan Harding from Severn House Large Print

SINK THE HOOD

SINK HMS COSSACK

SINK HMS COSSACK

Duncan Harding

Severn House Large Print
London & New York

This first large print edition published in Great Britain 2002 by
SEVERN HOUSE LARGE PRINT BOOKS LTD of
9-15, High Street, Sutton, Surrey, SM1 1DF.
First world regular print edition published 2001 by
Severn House Publishers, London and New York.
This first large print edition published in the USA 2002 by
SEVERN HOUSE PUBLISHERS INC., of
595 Madison Avenue, New York, NY 10022

British Library Cataloguing in Publication Data

Harding, Duncan, 1926 -
    Sink HMS Cossack. - Large print ed.
    1.   Cossack (Ship)
    2.   World War, 1939 – 1945 - Naval operations, British - Fiction
    3.   War stories
    4.   Large type books
    I.   Title
    823.9'14 [F]

ISBN 0-7278-7158-7

Printed and bound in Great Britain by
MPG Books Ltd, Bodmin, Cornwall.

Author's Note

They called them 'HO men'.

Today, half a century or more later, no one knows who they were. But back in the early 1940s, when the Nazi blockade had brought an island Britain to its knees and even that working-class staple, fish and chips, which had fed the nation through the Great Slump, was in short supply, those 'HO men' virtually saved Britain.

They were the 'hostilities only' sailors: boys barely out of their teens, who had been recruited to the Royal Navy just for the duration of the war. Many of these green, would-be sailors came from the coastal areas of the south-west and the north-east, but only one in fifty of them had ever been to sea. And of those who *had* 'been to sea', much of their sea-going experience was a trip on a pleasure boat on an Easter Bank Holiday!

Yet as more of the pre-war veterans of the regular Royal Navy were swallowed up by the cruel sea, with which a sailor fights a permanent battle, and killed by enemy action, the 'HO men' took over. In the last half of the

Second World War, they fought the great convoy battles of the Atlantic and the Mediterranean and those against the Japanese in the Pacific. Still 'wet behind the lugs', as the surviving regulars characterised them, these youngsters were the ones who crewed the landing craft which took the 'brown jobs' ashore at Sicily, Normandy and half a dozen other hotly contested beaches.

Now those who survived are old and forgotten. They shouldn't be. In particular, the 'HO men' who manned HMS *Cossack* deserve to be remembered. For the crew of that destroyer reflected the stubborn, gallant fight put up by the Royal Navy in those first two dark years of war when it appeared that Britain and all she stood for might well go down in bitter defeat. For a while the gallant rallying cry of one of their young officers put backbone into the nation once more, gave it hope, and helped through the long years to come before victory was finally achieved: a victory that so many of those 'HO men' would never live to see. It was simple, corny, old-fashioned, but it worked. It was:

'CHEER UP LADS ... THE NAVY'S HERE.'

1939

Roll out the barrel...
For the gang's all here.
Popular marching tune, 1939

One

They were auctioning the personal effects of the dead of a gunboat sunk by Jerry Stuka bombers in the Solent as the draftees crowded forward to the drafting notices. 'Come on, me lucky lads,' an old chief was crying, voice thick with years of cheap rum and Woodbines, 'see what presents old 'itler has got for yer ... Dirty cheap, maties ... Come on now, lads. Let's be having yer.'

Watching them, the two three-stripeys who were going to accompany the draft to HMS *Cossack* shook their cropped heads in mock wonder. 'What a shower,' the taller one said. 'Still wet behind the lugs. And they call themsens matelots. I've shat better sailors than them!' He hawked and was about to spit in contempt, then remembered where he was and refrained.

The other three-stripey said in a softer voice, 'Now then, Chalky, have a bit o' heart. They ain't so bad – and remember, they're all *volunteers*.' He emphasised the word as if it was important.

Chalky checked to see if the tab end was secure behind his right ear and then sneered, 'What did I tell yer. Still wet behind the lugs. Fancy volunteering!'

In the corner, the grizzled old chiefie, holding the auction of the dead sailor's effects, pulled out a pair of sailor's underpants, with a great hole in the seat. 'Now then, you youngsters,' he said, 'what am I bid for these drawers cellular, seaman, for the use of?' He grinned at his own use of official Royal Navy terminology. 'Best tropical quality. Why, you can see they've been fitted with the latest RN air conditioning.' He held them up for all the grinning young men to view.

But his offer fell flat. The bright-eyed eighteen- and nineteen-year-old rookies were not interested in the effects of the dead sailor, who was unknown to them, even if the underpants *were* fitted with the 'latest RN air conditioning'.

Death was for someone else. They were young and alive. Life was just starting for them. Already they were dreaming of being posted to some majestic battlewagon, with showers, cinemas, proper dining rooms, even – or so it was rumoured on the lower deck – with officer-type doors on the heads. In a ship of that kind they'd sail forth to do battle with the pride of the Jerry navy – the

Bismarck, the *Scharnhorst* and the like – to return victorious with the marine bands playing, the civvies cheering and laden down with gongs to be spoiled – and everyone knew what that meant – by the adoring Judies.

But on this particular bright October afternoon, with the war nearly six weeks old, the young men would be disappointed. For they would never serve on the great battle-wagons. Their fate had already been decided. They had been posted to the Fourth Destroyer Flotilla in the far north – not that that would play much role in their short brutal lives. They would hardly ever see their remote anchorage on the Forth, in particular those of them who were being drafted to a ship which they had never heard of up to now.

'What kind of ship is she, Chief Petty Officer?' they asked the Chiefie, who was now finished with his auction and was five pounds, five shillings the richer, too: a fact that made him exceedingly happy and would keep him happily drunk for the next two days.

'What kind o' ship is she?' he echoed with the professional joviality of his kind. ' 'S a bloody good ship, that what she is.' He beamed around their eager young innocent faces with his red-rimmed watery gaze.

'Spanking new. Top class. Too good for you shower of HO men, thinks old Chiefie.' He poked a finger like a hairy pork sausage at his barrel chest to make sure that they knew who he was talking about.

'Yer served in her yersen, Chiefie?' one of them asked in a broad Yorkshire accent, though he didn't look like that traditional Yorkshireman, 'big in t' body and weak in t' head', as the latter often commented.

'Not on yer nelly,' the chief answered. 'Wouldn't catch old Chiefie serving on one of them *Tribals*.'

'Why not, Chiefie?' the Yorkshireman persisted, obviously unabashed by the petty officer's rank and the row of medal ribbons dating back to before the Great War.

But the chief thought he'd said enough. He turned to the waiting three-stripeys. 'All right, you two.'

'Petty Officer.' They snapped to attention.

'Take these lads to the Globe and Laurel. See that they pay for a pint o' wallop for yer and then enlighten 'em.' He glanced at his watch. 'The draft's train leaves at sixteen hundred hours. See the whole shower's on it or I'll have the two of you on the rattle.' He glared at the draft beneath his bristling brows. But mixed with the intended threat, there was a look of searching, as if he were, for some reason known only to himself,

14

trying to etch each and every one of their young faces on his mind's eye. 'And none of you go buggering off home to Mummy,' he said, 'or yer feet'll never touch the deck when I get me hands on yer.'

The sailor with the broad Yorkshire accent made a show of trembling wildly and commented in what he supposed was a shrill female falsetto, 'Oh, Chief Petty Officer, don't shout at us like that. I think I'm about to get me monthlies, you naughty chiefie.'

By the time the old grizzled chief had collected his thoughts and was about to bellow his reply at this outrageous sailor who had dared talk to him, a veteran of the Battle of Jutland, in such a manner, the two three-stripeys had ushered the grinning draft outside, as if their very lives depended upon it.

'The Tribals,' the taller of the three-stripeys said reflectively, as the second pint of scrumpy bought for him by the draft came his way along the beer-wet bar. 'Well.'

'Come on, Stripey,' the voice urged from the back of the packed bar, the youths' faces red and damp with sweat, wreathed with the blue smoke of too many Woodbines and Park Drives, 'cough it up. The war'll be over by the time you get finished.'

'Cheeky young bugger,' the older sailor said in a good-humoured manner, for, he reasoned, he'd get another pint of scrumpy from the scrogs if he played his cards right. 'Well, the Tribals are eleven destroyers. The *Maori* ... the *Sikh* ... the *Mohawk* ... the—'

'What kind of ships is them?' someone interrupted. 'Bloody darkie navy or something?'

The stripey ignored the comment and concluded with, 'The last is the *Cossack*, laid down in '36 at Vickers-Armstrong on the Tyne.'

Naturally there was a cheer from the Geordies and the cry, 'We don't need the rest of you Southerners. We Geordies'll win the flipping war fer yer.'

'Keep it down to a loud rumble,' the older sailor cautioned. 'We don't want the landlord slinging us out. Anyhow, the *Cossack* was commissioned last June, and she weighs in at nearly two thousand tons' displacement with eight 4.7 guns in twin turrets.'

There was an impressed whistle and the lad with the Yorkshire voice said, 'I bet that'd make yer eyes blink – to have a broadside of that up yer arse.'

'D'yer want to try – with *vaseline*?' someone offered and again the happy young sailors laughed and cheered.

'But what about our chances in this here *Cossack*?' a steady, if cheeky voice asked, in no way as impressed as the others were.

Suddenly, for no apparent reason, save perhaps the coolness of that cockney voice, the noisy young draft fell silent. They turned to look at the speaker, some with angry comments on their lips, as if they were irate that his question had put a damper on their mood. Others were abruptly worried. It seemed as if they had realised at that moment that this wasn't a game, an excuse for a free piss-up. They were going to war, in a ship they hadn't seen before, run by regulars who would prove to be a tight, inward-looking bunch, probably looking after each other and their special oppos, but leaving the draft to fend for themselves – and at sea, with all its dangers, natural and man made, that could be fatal.

The speaker was a tall young man, a head taller than the mostly Devon men around him. He was blond, while they were all dark, and his uniform fitted him to a T. Indeed, he was the very epitome of the smart sailor, straight off a naval recruitment poster, save that his skin-tight jumper suit, with its enormous bell-bottoms, pleated crosswise, was definitely non-regulation. Nor were the cuffs of his jumper, turned back to reveal a loosely hanging silver identity chain on one wrist and the full, flash glory of a large, chromium-plated watch on the other.

'You talking to me, you no-badge sprog?'

17

the taller of the two three-stripeys asked, his face revealing his contempt for the speaker, whom he had immediately put down as a wide boy and a typical ship's lawyer: a lower-deck troublemaker if ever he saw one.

'Obvious, ain't it?' the other man replied coolly. 'A sniff of the barmaid's apron don't affect me much – like it does some folk.' He nodded, as if indicating the older man's crimson-coloured face. Around him the young draftees giggled behind their hands like a class of schoolkids who had seen their beak caught out. But then they knew Wide Boy Wilson, the former East End barrow boy. He was the same age as they were, perhaps nineteen. But he'd been around, was a regular spiv. As Wilson always said, 'Yer don't take any bullshit from them old matelots. They've only stuck it out in the Royal fer so long because they was no room in the spike–' he meant the workhouse – 'for 'em, poor old frigging souls.'

Wilson gave the older sailor a fake smile and, reaching forward, handed him a green packet of Woodbines. 'Here y'are, stripey, tuck them Woods inside yer tiddley suit and tell us, mate.'

The three-stripey was appeased; he didn't even notice the familiar 'mate'. 'Well,' he said thoughtfully and slowly in the manner of his kind, who always seemed to have all

18

the time in the world. 'I think yer could see she's been a bit of a jinx ship ever since she was commissioned. I remember that back in the autumn of last year, when Mr Chamberlain was having them talks with Hitler and—'

'Get on with it, mate,' Wide Boy urged. 'Or the war'll be over by the time you get—'

In that same instant, his protest was drowned by the shrill urgent warning of the sirens at the other end of the barracks. Almost immediately all hell was let loose. Frantically the portly landlord of the Globe and Laurel started to ring the 'time' bell above the bar. At the other end of the four-ales bar, his wife, head submerged in a warden's helmet, began twirling her wooden rattle, crying, 'Watch out for gas ... watch out for gas,' while outside the naval pom-poms started pounding away at a tremendous rate.

But all the racket could not drown the roar of airplane engines getting ever louder, so that the whole world seemed to be filled with their evil threatening noise. As the sailors fought to get outside, some of them already fumbling with their gas masks, for they had all been warned that the Jerries would use gas straight from the start, the first stick of bombs straddled the street outside. The room rocked and shook like a live thing. The door flew off its hinges. Hot air, acrid and stinking of burned cordite, shot into the room. Glasses fell to the floor and broke.

And then they saw it. Glimpsed it would be a better description. The gunners among the draftees recognised that evil black shape with its Maltese crosses immediately. 'A Junker 188!' they yelled, as the two-engined fighter-bomber came hurtling down the street outside at rooftop height, its prop-wash lashing the laundry hanging between the houses back and forth in a sudden frenzy.

Lead spurted from the turret machine gun. They could see it coming towards them like glowing golf balls, growing faster by the moment. 'Duck!' the Wide Boy yelled urgently above the roar of the engines and the frenetic chatter of the machine guns and the pom-poms in the distance.

Too late!

The tall three-stripey yelled high and hysterical like a terrified woman in sudden pain. He flung his hands to his face, as if he wished to shut out the sight of that harbinger of death roaring by the shattered windows of the old naval public house. Blood seeped, red and steaming, through his fingers. He moaned. His legs went beneath him like those of a newly born foal. Wide

Boy tried to grab him. In vain. The three-stripey, blood-red hands still clasped to his shattered face, sank to his knees. He shook his head like a boxer trying to fight off a count of ten. In vain. He couldn't do it. He gave a barely audible moan.

'Hang on, mate,' Wide Boy urged. 'I'll get you.'

But that wasn't to be. The older sailor fell backwards with startling suddenness. His blood-red hands fell from his face ... to reveal two suppurating empty pits. Next moment his head dropped to one side and he was dead.

Numbly Wide Boy stared down at him, as he lay there crumpled and unreal in the mess of broken glass and splintered wood from the bar. He opened his mouth. No words came. In the distance the Junkers headed for the sea, followed by the chesty thump-thump of the Bofors anti-aircraft guns. The war had claimed HMS *Cossack*'s first victim.

Two

On the morning of 1 December 1939 the new draft of HO men for HMS *Cossack* marched smartly across the freezing dockside, weaving in and out of the piles of oil drums, ammunition, food stores and the hundred and one things that the Fourth Destroyer Flotilla needed. 'Bags o' swank!' the chief petty officer barked, his breath fogging on the icy morning air. 'Swing them legs ... open them legs ... If anything falls out, don't worry, I'll pick it up, lads ... Now, remember who you are ... BAGS O' SWANK!'

'I remember who I am,' Wide Boy sneered out of the side of his mouth to his neighbour, who was crimson-faced with the exertion of swinging his free arm right to the shoulder while laden with the usual draft kit. 'A frigging mug for volunteering for the Royal.'

'No talking in the ranks!' the eagle-eyed chief petty officer yelled. 'That man there, I've got my eye on yer ... Now swing yer arms, you bunch o' pregnant penguins!'

A bunch of old hands in faded blue dungarees, apparently repairing a reluctant pneumatic drill, spotted them. They raised themselves slowly at the spectacle of the column, marching like men weary with fatigue, their backs aching with their efforts. 'We're poor little lambs,' they intoned solemnly, their faces blank and wooden, 'who have gone astray, baa baa baa.' There was sudden animation in their expressions now at the 'baa, baa, baa'.

'Little black sheep who have lost their way, baa, baa, baa.
Gentlemen matelots, all are we, doomed from here to eternity,
God have mercy on such as we—'

'I won't have mercy on you, you idle matelots.' The CPO's tremendous voice cut into their mocking ditty. 'By Christ, I won't ... NOW SHUT UP ... AND BLOODY WELL GET BACK TO YOUR JOBS BEFORE I HAVE THE LOT O' YER ON THE RATTLE!'

That did it. They stopped abruptly and turned back to their task, which they hoped would fill in the rest of the morning till they could tuck into the 'pusser's bangers and mashers', which had been promised them on this cold day. But those of the draft who

23

would survive would always recall that ditty in years to come. It would seem to them like a plea against the fates, which hadn't worked.

At the side of their new ship, the CPO halted them. For a minute or two no further orders came from that tight mouth that seemed to be worked by rusty metal springs. It was as if there was a heart behind the chief petty officer's hard bitter exterior and that he was giving these callow young men time to view their new home: one which from now until their fate would be inextricably linked, for better or for worse.

HMS *Cossack* was an impressive-looking ship. Despite the wartime camouflage and the mess of crates, ammunition and oil drums which littered her decks – something no pre-war skipper would have tolerated – there was no masking the beauty of her lines and the power they expressed. Even the most unimaginative of the young men who now stared at her from the corner of their eyes – for the CPO had still not stood the draft at ease – was stirred. She seemed to live up to the name of the tribe to which she belonged – the Cossacks. They were fast, dashing, irregular cavalry, who charged in on their half-wild mounts hacking and cutting with their sabres, reckless and with no regard to their own safety, before

24

vanishing into the grey snowy mists from which they had so suddenly appeared like grey predatory wolves.

Well, HMS *Cossack* had something of that about her and, as Wide Boy's neighbour in the still ranks whispered out of the side of his mouth, 'I think she'll do us proud, old mate, don't you?'

Naturally, Wide Boy, being the wide boy he was, the cockney product of the East End slums, could never admit to being impressed; that would have gone against his tough London image. In the Big Smoke, you were never impressed unless you were some kind of foreigner or a nancy boy. So he sneered, damning in his faint praise, 'I've seen worse.' But in his heart of hearts, the young man, who had now two short years to live, *was* impressed. Looking up at those powerful sleek lines and the deadly guns protruding from her A and B turrets, he knew he had joined something of which even *he* could be proud.

'All right, me lucky lads.' The CPO's harsh voice broke into his reverie. 'Let's be having yer. The captain'll want to speak to yer later, as soon as yer've stowed yer gear.'

The captain was followed by only one other officer, his second-in-command, 'Jimmy the One'. He walked slowly down their rigid ranks, eyeing each man as if it

25

were important to do so. His eyes were stern, like those of the CPO, who was watching the draft like a hawk, probably thinking up dire punishment for anyone who let him down in the presence of the Old Man. But there was more intelligent compassion in Captain Sherbrooke's gaze, as if he realised already what suffering these men would soon have to undergo, and his little speech of welcome, if that was what it was, was dry and businesslike enough.

He mentioned that he hoped the *Cossack* would be a happy ship under his command and that they would be happy while serving aboard her. He realised that they had no seagoing experience but he imagined that they'd soon find their sea legs. For they would be soon needing them. Here Sherbrooke paused and said, 'I must warn you – and this is the truth, and no buzz – we shall be expecting action soon, and when that occurs I must know that I can rely on every man here. There will be no excuses and no second chances. The sea is cruel and war at sea is even more cruel, men.' His eyes flashed fire suddenly. 'Remember that.' He smiled and raised his right hand slowly to his immaculate cap in salute. 'Happy landings and good luck to each and every one of you. Chief Petty Officer, dismiss the men!'

'Sir.' The old CPO stamped to attention as if he were back at Pompey on the square.

'Draft ... draft!' he bellowed, sending the seagulls in the rigging rising abruptly, cawing in shrill protest. 'Attenshun ... DISMISS!'

They swung round as one and then there was the usual outbreak of coughing, farting and desultory chatter before they started to investigate their new quarters.

Wide Boy didn't follow the rest immediately; he'd never followed the crowd in his whole short life. Instead he let his gaze wander around the cluttered deck, noting the ammunition which couldn't be stowed below decks and the crates of tinned food which indicated a long trip, perhaps without fresh food. There were even crates of Bass Light Ale, which could indicate that their Lordships in the far-off Admiralty might have the great generosity of allowing the lower-deck men to have a free ration of beer. Again that was indicative to the enquiring mind of the young cockney that something was going on. But what...?

It was the same problem that occupied the minds of the captain and his Number One, a happy-looking regular in his late twenties, whom the skipper often used as a sounding board for his own ideas: something he was doing currently. Sitting in the wardroom,

27

feet over the edge of the somewhat battered leather armchair and sipping at his first pink gin of the day, Lt Commander Sherbrooke said with apparent casualness, 'There's something going on in the South Atlantic, Number One. I suppose you might have heard something about it?'

Jimmy the One gave his usual open friendly smile, one which was very useful when it came to acting as buffer between the skipper and the crew in tense situations. 'You mean the *Graf Spee*, sir, don't you?'

The captain eyed him over the edge of his glass and commented, 'You're too smart for your breeches, Number One.' He added, 'Yes, the *Graf Spee*. We're on twenty-four-hour alert as of today. I'll announce it later, as soon as we're loaded and the new draft have settled in.'

With Sherbrooke, the Number One had learned never to rush things, though it did go against the grain. Instead he adopted an oblique approach, telling himself that when the skipper had had enough of his chit-chat, he'd come round and tell him what was on his mind.

Outside whistles were shrilling, indicating that it was time for civilian dockers to knock off. It was illegal in wartime to sound whistles and the like save when there was an air raid, but the dockies were bolshy, the lot

28

of them; they did exactly what they liked, whether it was against wartime regulations or not. 'I say, sir,' Number One opined, waiting for Sherbrooke to make his move, 'those bloody dockies are refusing to play the game again. I swear they're communist to the man.'

Sherbrooke took a careful sip at the pink gin and said, 'I don't exactly think so, Number One. The way the straw bosses treated them when they were casual labour before the war, you can understand how they feel and act now that they've got the new bosses – and that's us – by the short and curlies. They're making the most of the new war.'

'Perhaps you're right, sir. But they're not the poor buggers who are going to get killed in it. It's those lads of the draft.' He frowned.

Sherbrooke ignored the somewhat bitter comment. Instead he remarked, 'What do you think our chances are, Number One?'

'Chances, sir?'

'Yes – of having a crack at old Jerry. I mean, we're the fastest of the Tribals, thirty-eight knots, if we push it. We could make the South Atlantic pretty damned quick, if we got the orders to go.' He leaned forward. 'Do you think we might be called upon to do so?'

It would have given Number One the greatest thrill of his whole naval career so far if he had been able to answer that question with a straightforward 'yes', and he knew the skipper was expecting a positive response; he too was only too eager to get into action. All the same, he realised he had a duty to warn the skipper against his impulses. So he said, 'We could do it under different circumstances, that is if we had the same regular crew that we had back in September. But we haven't, sir. They've been paid off and sent to other ships. What we've got is a large percentage of HO men – boys, I should say really.' He paused and puffed out his cheeks grimly. 'I mean, can we expect them to perform like the old hands would have done? After all, the majority of them haven't been to sea before – they're absolute greenhorns.' He paused and said no more. He could see by the look on the skipper's face that Sherbrooke was disappointed. All the same, the captain was sensible enough to realise he was right. For the latter swallowed the rest of his pink gin in an angry gulp and said, 'Damn you, Number One, I suppose you're bloody well right.'

The following day, Number One thought he had been proved right and was glad that he had risked the skipper's wrath by his plain speaking, for what later became known on the lower deck as the 'Scouse and Cod' affair seemed to prove they were dealing with men who had not yet realised that if they were going to survive what was to come, then they had to adhere to comradeship and teamwork.

It was about midday and they were out in the estuary practising their anti-submarine drill, with the captain suddenly ordering a simulated 'ping'. Immediately the experienced depth charge crews, all regulars, sprang into action with practised ease. The bulk charges flew high into the air at the *Cossack*'s bow and fell into her wake in a precise pattern. Muffled explosions followed, with the sea heaving and great spouts of whirling white water hurtling upwards, bringing with them myriads of dead and dying fish of all species.

Most of the fish fell back far off the destroyer's bows. But off the starboard side, the deck crew spotted several large dead cod flopped down within grabbing distance. In peacetime what happened next might well have been overlooked. But not on active service. As Lt Commander Sherbrooke snapped icily afterwards, 'The *Cossack* is not a fucking civvy fishing boat, Number One. It's one of His Majesty's fighting ships. Get on to it!'

Unfortunately for the morale of the *Cossack*'s crew, the gunnery team of A turret, who were on lookout duty, were quicker than anyone, off to capture a rich prize almost before anyone was aware that it was. Abruptly off the port bow where they were stationed, a huge silver-bellied cod floated to the surface and wallowed there just ready for the taking. 'Fish and taties tonight for my mess!' Scouse O'Leary, a red-haired Liverpudlian with a temper as fiery as his hair, chortled. He grabbed for the nearest boathook and swung the clumsy improvised fishing rod over the side, while on the bridge the captain fumed at the impudence of these HO men.

A moment later his anger grew apace as Wide Boy acted, pushing Scouse's boathook to one side and sweeping the great cod into an empty fire bucket. 'Hard luck, matey!' he yelled above the second pattern of depth charges exploding. 'Yer mean fish an' taties for *my* mess, don't yer, yer Scouse git!'

The Liverpudlian's pockmarked, foxy face flushed an impossible puce colour. He raised his boathook as if he might well bring it down over the grinning Wide Boy's head. 'You ... you ... bastard,' he stuttered, trembling with rage. 'Give us back our fish.'

Wide Boy showed no fear, although Scouse was known throughout the lower deck as a bully and dirty fighter, who'd dab his knuckles in pepper and rub them across his opponent's eyes to temporarily blind him in a fist fight. 'Come and take it,' he challenged as Jimmy the One clattered urgently down from the bridge to defuse the situation.

'You watch it, you cockney bastard – or I'll have you.'

'You and whose frigging army?' Wide Boy challenged him, a cocky smile on his handsome, cynical face, as if he were deliberately provoking the Scouse, though he knew nothing could come of it at this moment, for he could hear Number One hurrying across the deck behind him.

'I'll ... I'll...' Scouse stuttered even more as he raised the barbed boathook. 'I'll do you—'

'Stop this – at once!' Jimmy the One yelled.

For what seemed a long time, the two men faced each other, seemingly unaware of the officer. Then suddenly, Wide Boy apparently got bored with the whole confrontation. 'So yer want yer sodding kipper, do yer?' he demanded.

'It's mine!'

'Then you shall have the ruddy thing,' Wide Boy yelled. He swung the red bucket effortlessly. The big cod flew through the air, followed by a gallon or so of icy sea water. The fish slammed into the Scouse's face. He slipped and fell back, spluttering terrible obscenities. Even in that same moment that Number One yelled to the nearest petty officer, 'Take those two men's names and put them on the rattle!' Wide Boy strolled calmly to where Scouse lay in a pool of water and then strolled equally calmly back to the petty officer waiting with his notebook.

Behind him he left the still prostrate Scouse, weighed down by the heavy cod which Wide Boy had draped artistically across his soaked chest, swearing a terrible revenge.

Wide Boy had gained an implacable enemy on board HMS *Cossack*.

Three

'Had a bloody lovely evening last night agen, Alf,' the aged attendant, who brought in the coal buckets every morning and made the tea at ten thirty precisely, was moaning to Alf outside the Great Man's door. 'Tommy bloody Handley on the bloody wireless agen. I've read every ruddy book in the house and it was too dark to walk to the public library – and to cap it ruddy all, that air raid warden started rabbiting on about a chink in my blackout curtain!'

'Well, it's the war, Fred,' the unknown Alf replied, as if that explained everything, 'total war.'

'Total war my arse! Looks like another bloody Hundred Years War, as far I can see.'

There was the clank of buckets and the voices moved away down the long Admiralty corridor, leaving the Great Man alone with his thoughts yet again. They weren't pleasant.

The new First Lord of the Admiralty, Winston Churchill, knew that the rest of the country was calling the new conflict 'the Phoney War', in which nothing had happened since Poland had capitulated to the Nazis in late September. As far as the navy was concerned, and the merchant navy, too, that was not the case.

Churchill frowned at the mess of papers on the great desk, which had belonged to Admiral Vernon back in the 18th century, as he remembered the last bunch of statistics he had received from Intelligence. The Royal Navy had already lost two battleships and two armed merchantman cruisers, and the bloody German raiders (surface, as well as those swinish U-boats of theirs below the surface) were accounting for at least 20,000 tons of British shipping a week, yet there was little that the Royal Navy seemed able to do about it. For the great Home Fleet, the greatest in the world, was pinned down in home waters just in case the brand-new German capital ships ventured out to do battle. Admiral Godfrey, the head of Naval Intelligence, was of the opinion, one with which he, Churchill, concurred, that this time the Hun fleet would not remain bottled up in their North Sea and Baltic ports as they had done in the last show until their sailors had mutinied and brought about the downfall of the old Imperial dynasty. This time, sooner or later, that madman would send out his fleet to fight, however great the risk to themselves.

In the meantime the rest of the Royal Navy was spread very thinly over the world's five oceans, trying both to guard British merchant shipping and at the same time prepare to meet any one of Germany's new 'pocket battleships' which had managed to evade the British blockade of the German harbours and was ranging the oceans looking for easy targets.

Churchill sighed. He was glad to be back in office after a decade in the wilderness. How the navy had welcomed him with that famous signal *'Winston's back!'* All the same, he knew he had picked the hottest potato in the whole cabinet. The navy might restore his old lost reputation but, at the same time, it was the most likely position to break it almost irrevocably, if he didn't watch out.

Frowning a little at that particularly gloomy thought, Churchill dipped the end of his Double Corona in the glass of brandy which was placed close to his pudgy hand on the big desk. He took a grateful puff of the expensive cigar and, as the blue smoke wreathed about his bulldog head, he considered the matter of the potential German raiders.

Despite his habits and self-indulgences, Churchill had a very fertile mind for such an old man. Indeed, his long-suffering wife Clemmie always maintained to her children that 'Daddy's mind races so much that he changes it at least twice a minute'. In her case she meant it as a mild reproof. But in Churchill's position as a cabinet minister, the speed of his mental reactions was an advantage. Unlike his staid but much younger cabinet colleagues, he was more flexible, not so blinkered, able to 'roll with the punches' as he was wont to say whenever anyone took him to task on account of his speedy mental reactions.

Now he considered the problem. He already knew from Godfrey's Intelligence people that the new German pocket battleship *Graf Spee* was on the loose in the South Atlantic and picking off solitary British merchantmen who were not sailing in the protection of a convoy. He knew, too, that the Royal Navy hadn't the kind of boat down there which could tackle the German ship. The Hun might be small, but she *did* possess eleven-inch guns and she was just as fast, perhaps even faster, than the antiquated British cruisers with their eight-inch cannon.

Churchill's frown intensified and for a few moments he even forgot to puff at his cigar. But there had to be some means of tackling the *Graf Spee*. She had to have some sort of weak link. But what?

Outside, hovering above the Admiralty courtyard, one of the home defence barrage balloons started to sail by like a sluggish grey elephant, followed by faint cries. 'The bugger's got away ... Leading Aircraftsman, get on that bloody winch gildy ... you silly bloody erk! Move it, now!'

On any occasion Churchill would have been amused. He liked these exchanges between ordinary people, who were so remote from himself and his own lifestyle. For, as Clemmie often complained of him in private, 'Why, Winston's never even been on the Tube in his whole life. As for carrying money in his pockets – *never*! Mind you, he's never got any money to carry with him. *He's* always spent up!'

But now that departing barrage balloon, wafted on its way by a gentle wind and followed by the angry shouts of the winch team down below, gave Winston the idea that would result in his first triumph of the so-called 'Phoney War' of 1939.

The *Graf Spee*, he reasoned with ever-growing excitement, seized by the idea like the overgrown Harrow schoolboy that he was at times, was naturally well prepared for a long fighting cruise. But she couldn't go it totally alone. She'd need fuel and other supplies and, in due course, she'd need to

39

get rid of the prisoners she'd taken from the allied ships she would undoubtedly sink. This time, the Huns would observe the rules of sea warfare; they wanted no trouble with the neutral Yanks. So they'd take prisoners and prisoners were a nuisance on a fighting ship; they had to be got rid of. *By God, he's got it!* He thrust out his hand to punch the highly polished Victorian bell on his desk in order to summon Godfrey of Intelligence. Then suddenly he realised that he had still not replaced his false teeth after the sweet biscuit the attendants had served with the morning tea – it was a ceremony he forced himself to partake in although, like most of the elderly admirals in the place, he would have preferred a a stiff peg of rum instead of that damned insipid tea: the curse of the English nation. Hurriedly he reached out for his dentures, nestling somewhat obscenely in a glass of water, wiped them with his pocket handkerchief, replaced them, struck the bell and with his other hand slapped down the button of the office intercom to demand in that great voice of his, which was going to thrill and rally the nation in the hard black years to come, 'Summon Intelligence and Maps.' The die had been cast.

One hour later it had been done. The coded signals started to fly to and from the great wireless room at the top of the Admiralty building. With Winston Churchill's power-drive behind them, they sped to unexpected places, with which the Admiralty usually had no contact. Every South American embassy and foreign ministry was warned, cajoled, threatened. Venezuelan oil exports would suffer ... Argentinian mass sales of corned beef would be reduced ... There'd be no further British investment in the Chilean copper mines. British legates were urged to forget protocol and concentrate on sabotaging the Hun's navy; 'Passport Officers', British Secret Service officers thinly disguised as diplomats, were ordered to use as many 'horsemen of St George' as they wished to grease palms, to buy agents and information and to 'liquidate' their German opposite numbers in some piss-stinking back alley of the South American ports' red-light districts.

Nothing was overlooked. Every loophole was examined and, if necessary, filled by any means available, legal or otherwise. Suddenly, startlingly, the whole great eighteenth-century pile that was the Admiralty building was buzzing. There hadn't been so much activity in its long stately corridors since the days just before the outbreak of war in September. Staff officers, normally so restrained and snooty, actually ran up and down the

41

echoing corridors with their important-looking clutches of papers. Admirals strode back and forth, jaws jutting as if they were about to spring into action at any moment, puffing furiously at their pipes. Teleprinters clacked. Phones jingled. Morse keys tapped. Secretaries leaned against the walls, looking very wan and frail, and began to weep softly into their little handkerchiefs.

It was at the tail end of this massive clerical offensive that the signals began to flash to the Fourth Destroyer Flotilla at their remote anchorage. The recipients knew instinctively that they weren't very high on Winston's and their Lordships' priorities – 'after all, who knows where we are in this arsehole of the world?' as the flotilla's junior staff officers often growled – but they knew, too, that the messages, marked 'Priority', indicated that there was the possibility of action just round the corner.

'It's going to be a little war.' Lt Commander Sherbrooke indulged himself in the old boner as he read his own decoded signal from the London source. 'But it's the only—'

'*War we've got!*' Number One beat the skipper to it with a bellow of joy as the two of them considered the possibilities it opened up for HMS *Cossack*.

In essence they were being given a section of North Sea off the Norwegian coast leading towards the entrance to the Baltic, where, naturally, the Flotilla leader had exercised his right to take up his position with his own ship.

'Rank hath its privileges, Number One,' Sherbrooke commented without apparent rancour as they surveyed the area on the large map pinned to the wall of the wardroom. 'Still–' he smiled winningly at the other man and the younger officers grouped excitedly in a circle around the wardroom map – 'although we're not out there in the Indian Ocean or the South Atlantic where the activity is, if Winston's right, we'll manage to get a few crumbs of action out here in this *anus mundi* – if my schoolboy Latin has it right, what? So,' he concluded, 'the Flotilla sails on the tide tomorrow, filled with high hopes—'

'And plenty of wind too, sir, from the bloody pea soup that so-called cook served for lunch,' one of the more irreverent subs muttered.

The captain was too happy to reprimand him, so he ignored the comment and finished with, 'Well, gentlemen, let me conclude with the wish that we shall find *something* out there ... and–' his face was suddenly very serious – 'look after yourselves, and happy hunting.' Without another word, he reached for his cap and left the wardroom without looking back.

The heavy silence was broken a moment later by an exuberant cheer from the sub-lieutenant who had made the remark about the pea soup. It was joined by those of the others and Number One, looking around their happy young faces, thought they were the best that Britain could produce. Mostly they were not even regular, but the types who had 'mucked about in boats' in the Solent in those sunny weekends before the war: 'wavy navy' to the man. But regular and wartime officer or not, he knew they'd do everything expected of them. They wouldn't let the old *Cossack* down.

It was the same with the crew when he told the CPO to let the 'buzz' circulate that they might well be on active service soon. (He thought it was wiser to give them a little foreknowledge prior to the captain springing in on them and telling these young HO men what they were in for.) They reacted much the same as the officers back in the wardroom had. They showed no fear at the uncertainty of what was to come. Their faces reflected certainty and assurance and he heard more than one say to his oppo, 'The skipper'll see us through – and the old *Cossack* too, natch.' It was clear, in the short time they had been aboard the destroyer, that they had taken to the ship. Like any pre-war sailor, they saw *Cossack* as their home and her crew their family. Number One told himself they were shaking down. In a matter of weeks, once they were at sea on active service, there'd be hardly any difference between them and some old three-stripey who had 'served with Nelson', as the old joke had it. All save Seaman Wilson.

Number One came across the big blond cockney whom, he knew, the others called 'Wide Boy', standing by himself at the bow staring at the dull grey autumn seascape, eyes narrowed as if he could see something known only to him out there on that harsh watery waste. Number One paused and said, 'Penny for them, Wilson?'

Wide Boy started and then, swinging round, came to a semblance of attention. 'Oh, it's you, sir,' he said, somewhat stupidly. 'Penny, sir? Not much. I was just thinking, that's all.' He blushed abruptly.

'What?' Number One persisted, with his usual winning smile on his handsome intelligent face.

'This and that.'

'Go on. Tell me about – er – *that*.' It was meant as a mild joke, but Wide Boy, who was usually so quick off the mark, didn't seem to notice.

'Don't rightly know, sir,' Wide Boy answered slowly, almost as if the officer wasn't there and he was talking to himself. 'Just feel a bit ... er ... funny.' He shivered.

Number One looked at him curiously and realised he would never get into the young cockney's head. It would be no use persisting. So he said, 'Go and see the sawbones, Wilson, that's my suggestion. He'll give you a number nine.' The officer meant a purgative. 'That's good for clearing your, er–' he smiled – *'head!'*

'Yeah – me head, sir,' Wide Boy agreed and forced a smile.

Number One said, 'All right, carry on now,' and went on his way. But when he looked back he saw that Wide Boy was leaning against the rail once more, staring out to sea, wrapped in a cocoon of his own thoughts and apprehensions. For a moment he wondered what they were. Then he dismissed the matter. He couldn't take the burden of every young sailor's problems on board. 'There's a war on,' he muttered, using the phrase they all used these days to excuse everything.

Four

The tropical sun was peeping over the horizon to the east in a blood-red ball. Beyond it the still ocean shimmered in its first rays, outlining everything a stark dramatic black. Watching from the bridge with the rest of his officers, Kapitan zur See Langsdorff thought that the conditions were absolutely perfect for the impending kill. Still, one had to be careful. They were still within range of the Tommy flying boats stationed on the African west coast. He bent to the tube and said, 'Air lookouts, max attention.' To his surprise he found himself almost whispering, as if Herr Churchill was on the other side of the bridge listening. He laughed softly and turned to his staff. 'Well, gentlemen, another five minutes and another plump bird will fly into range. I'm sure there'll be English whisky in the mess instead of schnapps this evening at dinner.'

They laughed dutifully, noting the captain's confidence despite the fact there was not another German warship within two thousand kilometres of their present position.

All the same, the skipper had managed to lure two fat Tommy tubs into their 'spider's web', as Captain Langsdorff called it, and dispatch them even before they had really been aware of what was happening to them. Now, he was about to do the same with the Tommy *Huntsman*, a fat juicy merchantman carrying a valuable cargo – raw rubber, leather, wool and tea. It was a funny combination of cargoes, they had to admit. Still, they were all valuable raw materials and trading products urgently needed by the Fatherland.

Up in the top lookout post, above the bridge, the senior mate swung his Zeiss glasses round. There was a faint dark smudge on the horizon to port. Hastily he focused his glasses more closely. It was smoke. It curled upwards in the bright circles of calibrated glass and was followed almost immediately by the flat outline of a ship. Urgently the Obermaat hit his radio button and reported to the bridge what he had seen.

Suddenly all was controlled hectic activity. The gun crews stood by their deadly 11-inch guns. Fire control parties put on their asbestos masks. Aircraft gunners swung their 20mm quick-firers skywards. All was eager anticipation and nerve-jingling tension. The *Huntsman* was sailing directly into Langsdorff's 'spider's web'.

As the sun left the horizon and the water started to turn a beautiful mottled purple-grey, the British merchantman steamed on steadily, seemingly totally unaware of the lean grey dangerous shape of the German warship waiting for it. The men watching, hard-faced and predatory, could hardly believe their own luck. Surely the Tommies should have seen them by now? What were they up to this day? Still sitting around on the mess deck drinking that terrible weak tea of theirs? One would think they hadn't yet realised that there was a war on and didn't know of the fate of the *Newton Beech* and the *Aslea*, which had preceded them into Captain Langsdorff's trap.

Not that their fate worried the captain of the pocket battleship. Already his quick brain was working out what should be done once he had attacked the unsuspecting Tommy. Time was of the essence. The merchantman's radio operator had to be silenced at once. That was his first priority, once he had stopped the *Huntsman*.

And then?

Captain Langsdorff knew he couldn't decide that until he knew how many crew she had aboard. Already his own ship was

49

carrying over a hundred enemy prisoners. He was running out of space below decks.

'Bridge!' The sudden alarm cut into Langsdorff's thoughts.

It was the radio room below decks. 'Captain?'

'They've spotted us, Herr Kapitan,' the radio officer snapped hurriedly. 'Their radio operator is sending out—'

Langsdorff didn't wait to hear the rest of the message. He knew that the enemy radio operator had to be stopped immediately. If he weren't, he'd have the whole shitty Tommy fleet homing in on them. 'A turret,' he ordered.

'Standing to,' the disembodied voice of the gunnery officer replied immediately, 'sir!'

'Prepare to fire warning shot.' Langsdorff turned to the signals mate. 'Flags!'

'Sir.' The smart young man snapped to attention. 'Signal. Stop wireless transmission *immediately*. Otherwise we will fire.'

'Sir.' The signaller, his cap's tails streaming out in the sudden warm breeze, began to click off the Aldis lamp at once.

The captain turned back to the tube and queried, 'Radio ... what kind of signal is she sending?' He meant the *Huntsman*.

'Usual, sir. Mayday ... alarm ... warning—' He broke off abruptly. 'She's read our signal. She's stopped transmitting.'

'Thank you,' Langsdorff barked. 'Good job.' But even as he turned to focus his glasses on the slow-moving merchant-man, he wondered if those signals had been picked up by the Tommy bases in Africa. Standard operating procedure now would have been to launch the warship's seaplane to do an immediate reconnaissance of the general area. But that was not to be. The damned pilot had messed up the engine. She couldn't fly until the *Altmark* delivered the requested replacement engine. His mind racing, he said to his staff, 'Gentlemen, we've got to move fast. The *Huntsman* sent off a distress-and-alarm signal. The Tommies'll move fast, even if they do sit around all day on their skinny arses drinking their tea.'

He had added the coarse humour to put his officers at their ease. But the ploy hadn't worked. They continued to look serious as the *Huntsman* began to heave to. On the bow, small dark figures were running back and forth, throwing things overboard. Langsdorff knew what they were: the ship's secret papers. The merchantman's skipper was reacting more quickly than he had anticipated. He'd have to do the same.

'We'll put a boarding party on to her within the next hour. We shan't have the time to transfer cargo. Therefore we want to keep

51

her intact with her cargo until the usual arrangements can be made. Klar?'

'Klar, Herr Kapitan!' his officers answered as one. They had trained ever since their ship had been launched for this kind of operation; they knew their job without being told.

'Scuttling!' Captain Langsdorff barked. 'We've got to watch that the Tommies don't try to open the seacocks and scuttle her be—'

'Sir!' The cry from the lookout up above cut into the captain's instructions. 'Rowboat leaving target ship, sir. Reading zero red—'

Langsdorff didn't wait to hear any more. He knew instinctively what the Tommy skipper was up to. He was going to leave behind some indication of his present position – a buoy, marker, something like that – that the Tommy flying boats would be able to pick up easily later on during their reconnaissance flights and start their pursuit.

In one and the same movement, he hit the button and bellowed down the squawk box, 'Guns, knock that shitting rowboat out – NOW!'

'Jawohl, Herr Kapitan,' the young gunnery lieutenant in charge of the 20mm quadruple quick-firer battery answered, as if he were only too eager to go into action.

Hardly had Captain Langsdorff relinquished his hold on the 'squawk box' than the starboard guns opened up. Suddenly the seascape was transformed. The tranquil sea, bathed, it seemed, with oil, disappeared. In its place there was a furious whirling wall of smoke, punctuated by white dots which were 20mm shells and which were gaining speed by the second.

A myriad splashes of white angry water erupted around the *Huntsman*. They sped the length of the ship. Gleaming silver tears appeared along her plates. A moment later that maelstrom of deadly fire swamped the lone rowboat. Langsdorff had one last glimpse of a man throwing up his arms in melodramatic agony before he pitched over the side, obviously ripped to pieces by the time he hit the water, and then the boat vanished. In the next instant the tremendous lethal volley of fire ceased, leaving behind a loud echoing silence that appeared to go on for ever.

'Eighty-four, sir,' the senior petty officer reported to Langsdorff, as the two of them surveyed the surly collection of British merchant sailors lined up on the afterdeck under the watchful gaze of two young marines armed with machine pistols.

'Heaven, arse and cloudburst,' the captain cursed, 'that many!'

'Yessir; I've counted them twice,' the senior petty officer answered.

Over at the right of his crew, the middle-aged merchant skipper looked anxious, as if he understood German and realised that the German officer was worried by the number of prisoners he had just captured. Behind him, the crew carried away the crates and cases of fruit, drink, cigarettes and the like which would be distributed this evening among the crew of the warship. Like pirates of old they were about to share out their booty. But the British skipper was more concerned with what these new German pirates who sailed under their own black flag, the crooked cross of Germany, would do to his crew than with their theft of his 'goodies'. He said in careful English, 'Excuse me for speaking, Captain. But what do you intend doing with my crew?'

Langsdorff forced a laugh, though at that moment the crew was precisely the problem which activated his mind the most. 'Don't worry, Captain,' he said in his accented but excellent English. 'I am no Captain Bligh of the *Bounty*. I will not set you adrift in – er ... longboat. I shall take care of you.'

The merchant skipper breathed an obvious sigh of relief. He touched his hand to the tarnished gold braid of his battered cap and said, 'Thank you, Captain.'

Langsdorff smiled and didn't reply. Instead he snapped at the senior petty officer, 'All right, they've been searched. See they're taken below for the time being. We'll sort them out later.'

The NCO snapped to attention and started rapping out orders.

Langsdorff turned to the handsome young signals officer, the only senior member of the ship's crew who belonged to the Party. 'Well ... What did you find out?'

'They managed to get off a signal, sir, after all,' he answered. 'The bastards! They gave away our position. In my opinion, the culprits ought to be shot without trial. Or put the lot of them in their boats and sink—'

'Keep your opinions to yourself, Leutnant.' Langsdorff cut him short.

'But sir, they've betrayed us!'

'No, they haven't ... they have simply carried out their duties as loyal subjects of their king and country. Now, get about your duties. I need time to think.'

The young officer flushed, balling his fists, as if he were about to continue to argue. Then he saw the steely look in Langsdorff's eyes and thought better of it. He saluted, swung round on his heels and marched off, leaving his captain to stare for a few moments at the empty tropical horizon, as if he might find an answer to his problem in that vast watery emptiness. But in the end, he couldn't.

An hour later he had finalised his hasty rough plan. The prize crew would sail the *Huntsman* on a separate course to his ship. In two days they'd make the rendezvous with the *Altmark*. Then her crew and cargo could be transferred and the enemy could be sunk like his two previous prizes.

In the meantime he would attempt a deception. So far these three successes had been carried out in a triangle that the Tommies would soon recognise and in which they would carry out their counter-measures. So he'd give them another alarm in the same area to delay them. Hastily he worked out the plan with his senior officer. They would send a fake submarine report purporting to be from a British ship in a completely different area – they knew which ships they were from spies' reports – stating that the Tommy had spotted a 'Jerry U-boat'. Captain Langsdorff liked that 'Jerry' bit; it seemed very genuine. Then, as he told his second-in-command, 'We can hope and pray that the Tommies in Africa will divert their attentions long enough to that area for us to make our rendezvous and get rid of the *Huntsman* and her crew.'

'Jawohl, Herr Kapitan,' the older officer snapped dutifully, though in his heart he wasn't convinced. He knew the Tommies of old. He had fought them at Jutland in 1916 in the 'old war' as a Fahnrich, and they weren't as foolish as many of these new Germans, who had come to maturity with Hitler's takeover of power in 1933. The English were a cunning, devious people, capable of any trick, dirty or otherwise. Still he saluted and went off in a hurry to work out the details of the plan, leaving Kapitan zur See Langsdorff to ponder the future momentarily. He felt cautiously optimistic. It was all a matter of getting through the next forty-eight hours to the rendezvous with the *Altmark* without being discovered. Then he would be on his own again, commanding the pride of the German Navy, a ship that could outrun and outgun every Tommy ship currently in the South Atlantic. Carried away by a sudden wave of enthusiasm, he bent to the squawk box once more. He pressed the button and snapped, 'Hear this ... hear this ... To all members of crew. This night as a token of appreciation at our latest victory, every man in the crew will receive a special ration of cigarettes and English chocolate. There will be, in addition, for every crew member over the age of eighteen, two bottles of best German beer. This is granted to you on the specific orders of our beloved Führer.' He added the lie glibly. Then he raised his right arm stiffly, as if he were back in the Reich, and cried, 'A triple hail to our Führer. Sieg Heil!'

As one the thousand-odd crew members froze at their various stations, right arms raised stiffly, bass voices echoing that primitive salute. The *Graf Spee* sailed on to her doom.

Five

'First request, sir, is by Leading Seaman O'Leary. *Sir!*' the chief petty officer bellowed, voice filling the stuffy little office.

Number One, who had been seasick for two days and on 'medication' to cure it – that is, copious draughts of pink gin – held his head in his hands and moaned. 'Chiefie, please keep it down to a low roar ... Can't you see I'm dying?'

'Sir!' the CPO bellowed yet again and Number One gave up. In a shaky voice he asked, 'What's the charge?'

The CPO cried at the top of his voice, 'Leading Seaman O'Leary – cap off. Three paces forward. *March!*'

While Number One quivered at the noise, Scouse, cap tucked firmly under his right arm, stamped forward the regulation three paces, and for the first time the deathly pale officer noticed the red swelling at the end of Scouse's nose and what looked like the start of a black eye above it.

The CPO glanced down at the request

book while Scouse stared fiercely into the distance, hands clenched and white with repressed emotion. 'Leading Seaman O'Leary requests to see the first officer, sir, to obtain permission to carry out a grudge fight with Able Seaman Wilson.'

'Wide Boy?' Number One caught himself just in time and said hurriedly, 'Haven't they had enough in these last bloody weeks – all these storms, those Hun cruisers off Norway—' He stopped a little helplessly as he realised that the CPO wasn't really listening. All the petty officer wanted to hear was his decision. 'Why, O'Leary?' he demanded.

' 'Cos he half-hooked the end of me banger, sir. And it weren't purser's either. It were a real bought NAAFI banger.'

Number One, feeling his stomach heave threateningly again, looked pleadingly at the CPO and murmured, 'I haven't understood a bloody word, Chiefie. Can you translate into English, *please.*'

Chiefie did his best, though it was obvious from the look on his craggy, weather-beaten face that he couldn't understand what Jimmy the One was making such a fuss about; it was all pretty obvious to him. 'He says, sir, that he wants a grudge fight with the able seaman because the latter did wittingly–' he hesitated about the big word –

'steal *not* an issue sausage, but one bought from the NAAFI with his own money.'

Next to him the Liverpudlian nodded his affirmation until Chiefie snapped, 'Stand still in the ranks there, man!'

'Must you really make a fight of it, O'Leary?' Number One queried, wishing he could simply curl up with a big bottle of pink gin in his bunk and forget everything, especially the bruised leading hand's sausages. 'You look as if you've been at it already, anyway.'

Scouse ignored the comment. Instead he growled, in that virtually unintelligible accent of his, 'Yer see, sir, in the leading hands' mess we don't much go for pussers' sausages. They don't have proper ends, them pussers' bangers. So we club together to buy NAAFI bangers. They've got lovely crispy ends when you—'

'Get on with it, man,' the CPO barked. 'Issue sausages, you see, sir, don't have skins. So they don't make for tasty ends—'

'Yer, and that cheeky cockney git has been nicking me ends – that is, till I tackled him. Just walks up and when I wasn't looking he nicked 'em *twice*. Once I asked me oppo Sparks whether his Judy was really in the pudding club—'

Number One sighed, opened his mouth to reprimand the offended Liverpudlian and then thought better of it; he simply didn't have the energy or will power to do so.

O'Leary seized his chance to pour out his heartfelt grievance, speaking passionately and rolling his eyes like a man sorely tried by a cruel fate. 'Then he had the cheek to tell me what I could do with my sausage, right in front of all my mates and me oppo. It ain't right. You don't talk to a leading hand like that. So I got up and tried to take a poke at him and the cheeky sod—'

'SHUT IT!' the petty officer bellowed and Number One felt his head was about to shatter.

Number One said in a weak voice, 'Grudge fight, is it?'

'Yessir,' a somewhat chastened O'Leary answered. 'I demand it.'

'Demand away,' the officer said, while the chief petty officer glowered at the cheeky Liverpudlian, telling himself the Royal could do without these 'scouses'; they were born troublemakers. But then again, wide boys and spivs were too. 'All right, O'Leary, step outside a minute while I discuss the matter with the CPO.'

'Cap on! Salute officer! About turn!' Chiefie hammered out the commands so that Number One felt his head was like a punchball being slammed from one side of the little cabin to the other.

When O'Leary was outside with the door closed, the petty officer asked, 'What do you think, sir?'

'Not bloody much,' the latter admitted. 'What's the Old Man going to think when he reads the charge sheet?' He raised his voice. 'Did commit an act prejudicial to Good Order and Naval Discipline in so much as one ... etc ... did steal a NAAFI sausage, the private property of—' He moaned. 'The Old Man'll think we've gone barmy.'

The CPO ignored the comment. He told himself that was Number One's problem; that's what officers and gents were paid for – to think. Instead, he said, 'Begging yer pardon, sir, what we gonna to do? An' we've got to do something.'

'Why?'

'Because the two of them are bloody troublemakers and, if they get away with it – ship's lawyers. We know about O'Leary. That Liverpudlian bugger is one of the best gunners turned out by Whale Island, but if he gets shirty, we've lost him. Given half a chance, that lot from Liverpool'll desert at the drop of a hat.'

'And Wide Boy – I mean Wilson?'

'Same but different.'

'How do you mean, Chiefie?'

'Smart sailor. Very good on deck. But too

63

bloody smart for his own good. We still can't afford to lose him to the glasshouse or on the trot, though. With them HO men as they are, we've got to keep the good ones—'

'Say no more, Chiefie. So we'll let O'Thingamabob have his grudge fight, eh?'

'Yessir. Get it out of their system.'

'Who do you think'll win if I grant his request?'

The CPO gave an uncharacteristic shrug. 'Hard to say, sir. That Wide Boy's a big bugger, but Scouse is more cunning. Them Scouses all is. If you don't watch him, he'll pull a few dirty tricks. Thumb in the opponent's eye, punch in the kidney, elbow in his balls, the usual sort of thing.'

'Delightful little habits they have on the lower deck, Chiefie.'

The CPO looked down at the ashen-faced officer as if he were seeing him for the first time, his craggy old face very serious. 'Yer must understand, it's a hard life these lads live. No cups of china tea with their little pinkies extended. Down there it's dog eat dog.'

'You make it sound like something out of Nelson's time.'

'Ain't much different, sir. Then what do you think, sir? Is the grudge fight on or not?'

'It's on. Wheel Scouse in.'

Duly O'Leary was 'wheeled in'. Number

64

One put on his cap again, as regulations required, and read out the scribble in front of him, as if it were a message from the First Lord himself. 'All right, O'Leary. Request granted. Tomorrow, eighteen hundred hours ... upper deck. Understood?'

'Yessir. Thank you, sir.' Abruptly the Liverpudlian's face lit up. There was a sudden unholy light in his eyes. Number One didn't like it one bit. It hinted of underhand methods and the fighting of a fist fight that would have the celebrated Marquess of Queensberry rotating in his grave.

'Remember,' Number One said severely, 'I shall be present at the fight. I want everything to be fair, square and Bristol fashion.'

'Yessir,' Scouse lied glibly. 'I'll see to it.'

The aged CPO shot him a hard look. Lying bugger, he told himself. You'd take a blind man's stick away and whack him with it in the guts. Aloud he bellowed, making Number One's head ring again like Big Ben chiming midday, 'Request granted. Eighteen hundred hours ... upper deck tomorrow. Salute officer. About turn. Quick march...'

Number One slumped back in his chair. He could hear them stamping down the companionway, all heavy boots and swinging arms and too much noise. He groaned and, looking at his ashen face in the fly-blown mirror opposite, asked himself, 'Who'd be a ruddy first officer on the *Cossack* on a morning like this?' Then he remembered he'd have to see Wide Boy before the fight. When he did, he'd better warn him, for somehow he didn't think the tall ex-cockney barrow boy was in the same league as the Scouse when it came to under-hand fighting.

He need not have worried. For the two were not fated to have their grudge fight just yet...

The sighting caught the crew of the *Cossack* completely by surprise. They had anticipated another rough-weather day just outside Norwegian territorial waters, fighting the freezing cold and the churning seas, the only thing to look forward to the blood-warming daily tot of 'Nelson's blood', when the bright lights erupted on the far grey-heaving horizon.

For a moment the lookouts, which included Wide Boy, were puzzled. What did the flickering lights mean? Then the Wide Boy, with that big-city quickness of mind of his, tumbled to it. 'Unidentified object off the port bow!' he yelled.

On the *Cossack*'s bridge, Sherbrooke and Number One flung up their binoculars as one. A dark vague shape slid into their lenses. In that instant they couldn't identify the object. 'Can't be a Hun,' Number One had just commenced saying, 'because it's Norwegian territory waters,' when it started.

With the bansheelike howl of an express train rushing through an empty station at midnight, a great shell tore the sky apart and plunged into the sea some two hundred yards behind the destroyer. A moment later another fell out of the leaden, lowering sky and did the same. Crazily the *Cossack* rocked under the impact and for a moment it seemed as if the radio mast would hit the top of the water.

'Holy Mother of God!' the captain yelled. 'They're firing at us!' He pushed back the fur hat he had now taken to wearing in honour of his ship and peered more closely through his glasses, trying to make out the silhouette, while from below came the shocked voice of Guns reporting, 'All stood to, sir ... Ready to fire on instruct—'

The rest of his words were drowned by yet another salvo scorching towards the *Cossack*. Next moment she rocked wildly once again, but this time the shells landed short. Huge gouts of whirling wild water hissed upwards and obscured the unknown assailant for a moment. But they didn't need to see the target. There could be no doubt of who it was – a German, and a big one at that.

'They're ranging in, sir!' Number One yelled urgently as the *Cossack* came back to an even keel once more and he could relax his hold on the nearest stanchion.

'For God's sake, Number One, don't you think I know that?' the captain yelled back wildly, his fur hat sliding to the side of his head so that he looked somewhat like an old biddy in out-of-style headgear who had had too much stout. 'And she's a big bugger.' He hit the squawk box as down below the whistles shrilled their urgent warnings and the harsh klaxons shrieked. 'Guns, prepare to return fire.' He waited for the gunnery officer to confirm the order and then called the engine room. 'Smoke!' he cried above the noise and the roar of another ear-splitting salvo. 'Prepare to make smoke.'

Down on the swaying deck, there was controlled chaos. Fire-fighting parties ran to their duty stations. The deck gunners, pulling on their helmets and antiflash gear, were scrambling into the seats of their new Oerlikon cannon. Smooth and sinister, the turrets with their big 4.7 guns swung round to face the grey shape on the horizon which was the enemy.

Sherbrooke had one more duty before he commenced firing. He had already assessed his position and that of the enemy. He was outside Norwegian territorial waters; the ship firing at him was within. Now he cried, 'Sparks!'

The ever-present smart yeoman of signals was there, as usual, with his message pad at the ready. 'Sir?'

'Send a signal. To their Lordships. Am being attacked by unknown enemy ship from inside Norwegian territorial waters. Am about to engage. Get that off *now*.'

'Sir.' The yeoman pelted across the bridge in a fashion that the captain would never have approved of under other circumstances, heading for the radio shack, while the latter poised over the box, ready to give that fatal order for the first time in this new war – 'OPEN FIRE!'

Watching and waiting, Number One realised suddenly with the one hundred per cent certainty of a vision that what happened next would change his whole life – and that of everyone else on board HMS *Cossack* at this moment. There was no going back now.

Next instant Captain Sherbrooke gave his momentous order. With a great crash, the destroyer's 4.7 inch guns opened up. For HMS *Cossack* the war had commenced at last.

Six

Churchill clapped his hands together like a small child given some extra special present. 'Excellent ... excellent!' he cried to the po-faced civil servant who had brought in the news, while in the background Admiral Godfrey, Head of Naval Intelligence, grinned. 'That's the stuff to give the troops!'

'Yessir. Clearly, sir,' the civil servant in his high-winged collar, black jacket and striped pants agreed with little apparent enthusiasm. 'But there is the matter of international waters to be considered. I've already been in touch with the FO and their people are a bit worried about Norway's position in this matter.'

'Bugger the Foreign Office – and for that matter, bugger Norway too. We all know the Norwegians are playing a double game. They pretend to be neutral, yet they're letting the Huns use their railways and other facilities with impunity. I fancy we'll have to invade the country soon, if they don't stop.'

The civil servant's mouth dropped open,

aghast. 'But Mr Churchill—'

'Don't Mr Churchill me,' the First Lord snapped, fire in his gaze now. 'Off you go and deal with the FO. Keep them off my back and let me and my good chaps of the Royal Navy get on with winning the war.'

For a moment it seemed that the civilian might refuse to go, but then he saw the look in Churchill's eye and thought it was wiser to do so. Troubled and muttering to himself like a man sorely tried, he left.

'Now, Godfrey, what news?' Churchill asked as soon as he had closed the door behind him.

'A great deal, sir.'

'Speak, oracle,' Churchill said in high good humour.

'Well, sir, it looks as if the *Cossack* has tackled either the *Gneisnau* or the *Scharnhorst*. The Huns are going wild. They want the action broken off immediately, but the *Cossack* won't let them. Her skipper's after them although he's hopelessly outgunned.'

'Good for him. Naturally the Huns don't want to draw attention to their iron ore supplies coming from Narvik and the like in the north of Norway.' He beamed at the Intelligence officer. 'We'll give Herr Hitler one in the eye and then people will stop all that idle talk of the Phoney War. I could strangle that American senator for ever

71

having invented the damned phrase.'

'There's even better news, sir,' Godfrey went on, infected by Churchill's sparkling mood. 'We're on to a much bigger fish in the South Atlantic.'

Churchill's eyes gleamed even more. 'You mean the *Graf Spee*?'

'I do indeed, sir. She tried to fool us with false alarms, etcetera, with which I won't bother you. But we didn't fall for it. Now we know that she has a supply ship called the *Altmark* returning back to the Fatherland. So we can assume that she—'

'Has been resupplied' – Churchill's agile mind beat him to it – 'and is ready for one last fighting cruise before she, the *Graf Spee*, does a bunk herself back to that same Fatherland.'

'Exactly, sir.'

'So what now?'

'It's fairly obvious what the *Graf Spee* will do before she makes that dash home, sir.'

Churchill didn't make the cynical comment that had just sprung to mind; he was too overjoyed at the news to make fun of the vice-admiral for being so confident he could read the Hun captain's mind. Instead he remained silent – a difficult task for him – and waited to hear what Godfrey had to say.

'She'll run along the South American coast – by now the African coastline's too

72

hot for the *Spee*, since we've spread the rumour there for Hun agents to pick up that we're assembling a huge task force including two carriers to hunt her down in that region.'

Churchill nodded his understanding, but still didn't interrupt.

'So we feel that we can deal with the *Spee* off the South American coastline before she makes that mad dash across the Atlantic for a home port. If we do corner her and she won't fight, we'll have the psychological victory of having the *Spee* bottle herself up in one of those banana republic ports till the end of the war.'

Churchill shook his massive head. 'Yes, Godfrey, but I prefer an outright victory. But now I'll tell you what *I* think she'll do.'

Godfrey sighed. He knew it would come to this; it always did. Amateur that he was, with no naval experience, Churchill always thought that he knew better than the experts. Still, he knew his own fate depended upon humouring Churchill's whims. So he said, with an air of resignation in his voice, 'Please do, sir.'

'The Hun captain won't do the obvious. After all, he has the run of the South Atlantic *and* the Indian Ocean until we can assemble a force strong enough to tackle him. He'll feint to the Indian Ocean, deal with whatever easy pickings he can find then, feint again as if he is heading for South America – and why should he go the whole hog there? He'll know those neutrals won't dare risk our wrath and trade embargos by helping the Germans. Halfway there, while we're readying ourselves to deal with him off South America, he'll turn about and go all out with the last of his fuel and provisions for the Fatherland.'

Churchill paused and, breathing a little hard with the effort of all that concentrated talk, reached for his jigger of brandy.

Godfrey was quite impressed in spite of himself. 'I get your point, sir,' he said slowly, as he absorbed Churchill's argument. But suddenly he felt deflated and worried. He said, 'Although the *Graf Spee*'s days *seem* numbered, at the moment her captain has the drop on us.'

'Exactly. He has the advantage of interior lines of communications. He can zip hither and thither while we're assembling forces spread over three oceans to deal with him – and for a week or so, he can outfight us wherever we chance to encounter him. It's one of the disadvantages of being a world power with at least a two-ocean navy.'

Godfrey understood that argument; it was one that had worried British naval planners and strategists ever since the end of the

Great War. 'So it means we should be pre-pared to encounter the *Spee* every-and-any-damn-where until we can finally crush her with overwhelming power.'

'Yes.'

'And your suggestion, sir?'

Churchill favoured him with a cheeky grin of the kind he must have used as an inky-fingered schoolboy cocking a snook at his teachers at Harrow half a century or so before. 'I've already advised their Lordships of my thoughts on the subject, Godfrey. We pull back everywhere in the North Atlantic. A stopgap measure. If the *Graf Spee* does manage to escape from her present raiding cruise, we'll be waiting for her at the entrance to the Baltic. There she'll have to pass through the eye of the needle, and she won't be able to make it.'

'Does that mean the *Cossack*—'

'It does. We'll need every ship we can muster, from battleship to – er – pinnace. We can't let Herr Hitler cock a snook at us now on our own home ground. He's dealt with Poland while we sat on our damned thumbs.' Churchill's round face flushed with righteous indignation. 'He won't get away with it again, Admiral. The *Cossack* comes back like the rest...'

'Pull the other frigging one, it's got frigging

75

bells on it, Stripey,' Scouse snarled angrily over the noise in the hot fetid turret. The extractor was going full out and to the rear of the steel box the hydraulic lift was bringing up a load of shells for which they were waiting.

The reservist whose forearms bore the scars he had suffered at Jutland as a boy seaman tugged at his flash hood and shouted back, 'We're well out of it, son. That Jerry's a big bugger. Once the skipper lets down his guard fer half a mo, she'll get our proper range and the Jerry'll make mincemeat of us.'

'Let him frigging try.' Scouse peered through the telescope once more, across the grey-heaving sea, at the dark smudge which was the enemy battleship. Screwing up his red-rimmed eyes, he could just make out the cherry-coloured flames aft. The last salvo he'd fired had hit the bugger, all right; there was no mistaking that. Now the word had just come down from the bridge that they were to disengage, and that meant they would cease firing. It wasn't frigging fair.

Relaxed now, the old reservist and his mate loaded another heavy 4.7 inch shell into the gleaming silver metal slide that would insert it into the gaping breech.

He took his time now, whereas the moment before he had been working flat out like 'a bloody fiddler's elbow', as the reservist had expressed it himself. The pressure was off.

But not for O'Leary. He had been the best gunner turned out by his course at Whale Island gunnery school. But that had just been practice. Now, with that usual half-Irish anger that motivated most of his actions, he burned to knock out a real ship. It wasn't that he was after promotion or gongs; he was motivated solely by his love of a scrap and the desire to hurt. It was something that had got him into pub fights every weekend ever since he had been old enough to go into them. 'Are you sure that we're gonna let the Jerry get away with it?'

'Dead sure. The gunnery officer said.'

'Nancy boy with his silk scarf and gold cigarette case! What does he know?' Scouse sneered, never missing a chance to jeer at someone, especially if that someone were in authority above him. 'One more salvo and with a bit o' luck we'd hit her ammo locker and that'd be bye-bye Jerry.'

The reservist didn't reply. He'd seen Scouse's kind before. They never survived. All full of piss and vinegar. He, for his part, was going to survive to go back to the old woman, his baccy and his Saturday evening pint and dominoes at the local.

Up on deck, Wide Boy didn't feel the same

sort of blind aggression which animated Scouse, his enemy. He had a full oversight of the damage the Jerry's guns had inflicted on the much smaller craft. So far the *Cossack* hadn't taken any direct hits. But there had been several near misses with shrapnel whizzing lethally across the decks, slicing through steel hawsers as if they were strings; peppering the plates and ripping them into shining shreds of torn metal; inflicting terrible wounds on the deck crew. Here and there shapes were still moving and moaning among the dead, lying there like bundles of abandoned wet rags, while a frantic sweating surgeon-lieutenant, his arms blood red to the elbows, worked all out among the human misery.

Wide Boy, sweating too despite the biting cold, was helping him, though it wasn't his job, but most of the HO men on deck were frankly scared of dealing with the dead and dying. They held back or found other jobs with the fire-fighting teams trying to deal with the flash fires that were now blazing everywhere. Wide Boy, however, knew that somebody had to do the job; and now he worked with renewed energy, for he had just heard the new buzz. The skipper had been ordered from Whitehall to disengage. He was all for it. Some of the wounded, he knew, wouldn't survive if the surgeon-lieutenant didn't get them to a proper shore hospital soon.

Steeling himself, his hands slippy and greasy with blood and gore, he dug his thumbs yet again into the young sailor's groin and tried to stem the blood that was jetting in a sparkling crimson arc from it. The steel shell splinter still jutting from the gaping wound had just missed the poor devil's balls. All the same he was going to die, a desperate Wide Boy knew, the kid was going to die if he didn't stop the bleeding soon.

'Come on, come on!' he cried desperately as he exerted all his strength on the unconscious sailor's abdomen, 'stop fucking bleeding, will yer ... stop it *NOW*!' Gritting his teeth with the effort, opaque beads of sweat trickling down his fiercely wrinkled brow, he willed the boy to do as he wished.

It was at this moment of personal crisis for the young ex-cockney barrow-boy that it happened. Scouse snapped.

'Fuck this for a game of soldiers!' he cried to no one in particular, 'I'll get the Jerry bastards yet!' Before the petty officer in charge of the turret while Guns was up top speaking to the captain could stop him, he pulled the firing bar. The great gun crashed home, sliding smoothly along the recoil system. The ship gave a slight lurch. In the next instant the shell was winging its way to the steel monster vaguely seen on the horizon.

While all about him fellow gunnery crew members cursed or cried out in astonishment, Scouse, face inflamed with rage, counted off the seconds till impact. 'One ... two ... three—'

He gasped and stopped. On the horizon there was a sudden burst of blinding light, followed an instant later by a mushroom of thick black oily smoke rising rapidly into the leaden sky. The German ship lurched. He caught a glimpse of a radio mast tumbling downwards, accompanied by a trail of angry blue electric sparks, and then the *Cossack* was wheeling round and thick black smoke was pouring from the stack. The captain had ordered the ship to disengage. *Cossack* was on her way home and Scouse was suddenly realising he was in trouble. He had fired without orders. The old stripey who had been at Jutland muttered, almost as if to himself, 'Now you've torn it, Scousey, lad ... They'll hang yer from the sodding yardarm for this little lark...'

Seven

The first German star shell curved into a burning arc above HMS *Ajax*. She stopped and prepared to fire back, for her engine room was already badly damaged in the uneven fight and she had lost power rapidly. If she could plant an exact salvo on the *Spee*, she might just exact her revenge. But that wasn't to be. A great white searing flame hissed like a blowtorch along the *Ajax*'s deck.

What happened next will be etched on the minds of the onlookers for ever. Those who survived – and there were, unfortunately, many casualties – will never forget it. Suddenly the planks of the deck erupted into a mass of roaring flames, a veritable inferno. Here and there crewmen were turned into flaming torches. They flung themselves overboard in their agonised torment...

Churchill gave a little sob. He could read the Reuter correspondent's report no more.

The First Lord had the imagination of a novelist. He could well visualise those poor British sailors. Being devoured greedily by the flames ... swallowed by that all-consuming scarlet monster ... Their white flesh being transformed into a horrible black bubbling pulp ... The blackened crust cracking to reveal the vivid scarlet flesh beneath ... He dropped the report to the floor, while Admiral Godfrey watched him a little helplessly, wondering when it would be opportune to tell a very sad-looking Winston the good news.

Churchill clenched his pudgy fist in and out, as if motivated by some terrible rage, which he was barely keeping under control. 'Those damned frocks,' he hissed through gritted teeth, as if speaking to himself. 'With their penny-pinching policies and all that socialist guff about peace and goodwill to all men ... Now they condemn our poor young men to fight and die in antiquated ships against Hun craft that are the most powerful in the world. When, oh when will we English ever learn!'

For one horrid moment Godfrey thought the First Lord would break down and start sobbing. 'Sir,' he broke in.

Churchill looked up, his eyes brimming with tears. 'Yes?'

'Excellent news, sir!' Godfrey forced himself to smile and put some enthusiasm into his voice. 'Best we've had in many a long week.'

'What?' Churchill asked numbly.

'From the South Atlantic, sir.'

'Go on.'

'Sir, after that unfortunate business with the *Ajax*, about which you've just read—'

Churchill nodded, but said nothing. Outside it had begun to snow, soft flakes that came down gently, almost imperceptibly. It was the first snow of that winter.

'Well, Captain Langsdorff of the *Graf Spee* has made a bad mistake.'

For the first time that morning Churchill's eyes lit up. There was new hope on his round face. 'Go on.'

'The *Graf Spee* rushed at high speed for land, heading for the Uruguayan port of Montevideo on the River Plate. Came in at thirty knots or more. Didn't even wait for a pilot boat to see her in. Now she's trapped on that river, licking her wounds I suppose.'

'Praise God! Now when she attempts to come out, dammit, we'll be waiting for her with every ship we can muster—'

'And the other bit of news, sir,' Godfrey interrupted the First Lord's excited outburst, 'is that we've got a fix on the *Altmark*.'

'Yes?'

'She's in port in Cadiz. You know that she

83

feels safe there. The Spanish fascists are supposed to be neutral, but they fall over backwards for the Huns. Anyway, our agents there tell us she'll sail when she thinks she's thrown us off the scent. Then she'll probably make a dash for Southern Ireland – another safe haven, thanks to the IRA – and from there to the Baltic ports.'

Churchill, numb up to now after having read that terrible Reuter's dispatch, started functioning at full speed once more. 'Devil's spawn!' he spat. 'The *Altmark* and every other Hun ship connected with that *Graf Spee* must be blown out of the water. Gib must be alerted at once. Pompey, too.'

'Already been done, sir,' Godfrey assured an electrified First Lord.

'Excellent.'

'But there's one catch, sir.'

'Pray what is that, Godfrey?'

'We've just learned that the *Altmark* is packed with our prisoners. The *Spee* was filled with them and before she made this last run for safety, she got rid of them to the *Altmark*.'

'That means we cannot simply attack her,' Churchill said thoughtfully. Outside the snow was increasing in strength. Now it was pattering against the large windows of the Admiralty audibly. Churchill shivered, but it wasn't with the cold.

Godfrey waited.

Finally Churchill broke the heavy brooding silence of the place and said, 'We can assume that the *Altmark* will use all the fuss occasioned by the *Spee*'s last attempt to come out and fight. Her skipper will reason that all attention will be directed to South America and that will take the pressure off. Then she'll attempt to make a run for the Baltic.'

Godfrey nodded his agreement.

'But we won't take our attention off her. We'll watch Cadiz night and day, just like that old pirate Sir Francis Drake did before he tackled the Spanish fleet – *illegally*.' He chuckled at the thought.

Admiral Godfrey looked alarmed. Like most sailors, he only acted unconventionally when he was at sea. On land, sailors, especially high-ranking ones, were all too conventional. 'You're not going to do anything – er – *wrong*, sir?' he queried carefully.

Churchill chuckled again.

Godfrey's look of alarm increased at the tone of Churchill's voice. He knew it of old. There was trouble brewing.

'We shall do what we want, Godfrey. The only problem is getting caught doing it. If we aren't, well—' He shrugged. Then his jocular look vanished and he added grimly, 'But first we must make the *Graf Spee* and her Huns pay for what they did to our poor tars. First the *Graf Spee.*'

Godfrey looked out at the flying wall of snow and the grey ominous sky beyond. He told himself he would not like to be in Captain Langsdorff's shoes now. If Churchill had his way, the German skipper wouldn't last out long enough to see 1940...

1940

Where was the engine-driver when the boiler bust?
They found his bollocks and the same to you.
Bollocks...

Popular marching song of 1940

One

'I've got spurs that jingle-jangle-jingle ... as I go riding merrily along,' the cookhouse-wallah repeated with monotonous regularity, as with the rest of the deck watch he gazed at the four-engined German reconnaissance plane *Condor*. It had been circling the *Cossack* and the rest of the little convoy ploughing its way steadily northwards for a quarter of an hour. Indeed, Number One had got so damned annoyed at the plane, which was keeping just outside the range of their anti-aircraft guns, that he had signalled, 'Please go round the other way ... You're making us dizzy.' The reply had come back quickly enough. It read, 'Kiss my arse!' and had made Number One smile despite the fact that he was 'bloody well cheesed off at her', as he had snorted to the *Cossack's* new captain, Vian, a keen-faced energetic officer who had gingered up the *Cossack* since he had taken over recently.

'Put a frigging sock in it, Cookie,' Wide Boy, now a full AB, snorted. 'I've had

89

enough of that bloody jingle-jangle of yourn.'

'Just trying to keep the crew's spirits up,' the cookhouse-wallah replied, flinging another peeled potato into the huge wash-tub of potatoes in front of him on the deck. 'It ain't no fun spud-bashing for hours on end.'

Wide Boy gave up. He had his duties to attend to anyway, especially keeping an eye on Scouse, who had been demoted to ordinary seaman after the incident in A turret and was now relegated to ordinary deck duties: something that rankled. For, as he would whine to anyone prepared to listen, 'Frigging best gunner of my term at Whale Island and now all I am is a frigging broom-jockey swabbing decks.' Not that many people were prepared to listen to his complaints – especially Wide Boy, who had a problem of his own, one which he hoped every morning that dawned would go away. So far it hadn't.

But this particular early February morning, he had no time for his personal problems. This part of the deck and its safety was his priority. For he knew that damned Condor, circling, circling and circling, as if it had all the bloody time in the world, heralded trouble for the *Cossack*.

Number One felt the same. He snuggled

his face, flushed a brick red with the icy wind that seemed to be coming straight from Siberia, deeper into the collar of his duffle coat and prayed it would soon be time to come off watch and escape to the fug of the wardroom. Even five minutes' heat would suffice. At least, he told himself, if I'm going to be hit on the head by a lump of Hun steel, I want to go to my watery grave *warm*! Not that the young second-in-command was going to suffer that fate – just yet. He would have his triumphs before that eventuality.

He forgot the cold and considered their position. They'd escort the coastal freighters as far as Scotland and then the *Cossack* would detach herself from the somewhat boring convoy duty and return to the base of the Fourth Destroyer Flotilla. Not, he told himself, that he anticipated this particular convoy being dull. If the current weather held, they could expect a dive-bombing attack by Stukas, or even one from the sea by German E-boats – they were too small fry for the Huns to waste subs on. But trouble of one kind or another would be coming their way.

He peered around the deck below. Everything seemed shipshape and Bristol fashion. The gunners had already closed up. They shuffled their feet against the cold, clad in their heavy duffle coats, eyes flashing to the sky. Behind the bridge, the rating who fired the battery of PAC rockets had closed up too. The rockets would carry thick wires aloft in the case of an aerial attack and – hopefully – entangle the Jerry dive-bombers. Not that the crew had much faith in the new device straight from the Admiralty. As they quipped, 'Might bring down a couple of seagulls if yer lucky – *weak 'uns*!' But Wide Boy, who they had thought would be the first to ask for a transfer or go on the trot, was turning out to be a tower of strength, though the cockney ex-barrow-boy refused to admit it. As he would retort when praised, 'Better than the frigging glasshouse!'

Vian poked his head into the bridge housing. 'Number One!'

'Sir?'

'We're picking up something on the radar. I'll be down in my day cabin doing some bloody paperwork. Give me the wire as soon as you spot trouble.'

'Sir.'

Captain Vian disappeared and Number One told himself they'd got a good 'un in the new skipper. If anyone could finally get them into proper action in this second year of supposed total war, it would be Vian. He was a fire-breather, craving action, though

Number One was sure that he wasn't a glory-hunter out for 'gongs'. Vian just felt that a regular sailor's job in wartime was to seek out the king's enemies and destroy them.

Time passed leadenly now. They surged forward, eyes blinking in the keen wind as they sought out what they knew *had* to come; for now the German reconnaissance plane had disappeared. But the enemy stubbornly refused to make an appearance. Indeed, Number One had almost convinced himself that they weren't going to have any trouble this day and had accepted a steaming hot mug of cocoa from one of the wardroom stewards when it happened and took him by complete surprise.

Even before the klaxons started to sound their urgent warnings and the petty officers began doubling back and forth, shrilling their whistles, the noise of the ship's engines were drowned by the roar of plane engines going all out. Suddenly, startlingly, all was noise, shouts, cries of alarm, orders.

Next to Wide Boy, an elderly reservist whipped out his false teeth, tucked them safely inside his tin hat, replaced it on his grizzled head and cried between teethless gums, *'Here ze cum!'* He threw off the safety of his chicago piano and prepared to meet the challenge.

Wide Boy swung round. Three Junker 88s were skimming across the sea at a tremendous rate. Their propwash whipped up the water in a fury. Almost instantly brown clouds of smoke peppered the air all around them. The German pilots, briefly glimpsed behind the gleaming perspex of their cockpits, flew on grimly. The first PVC burst into action. The steel rope was carried upwards. Wide Boy held his breath. Would the new device work? It hadn't so far.

The gunner struck lucky. The centre plane of the trio was hit. The chain and wire wound their way around the port engine. There was the unholy clang of steel striking steel. Wide Boy caught a glimpse of the horrified look on the pilot's face. Next moment the Junker lost power. At that height, the starboard engine alone wasn't sufficient. The plane tilted. The port wing hit the sea. Like a giant cartwheel, the Junker spun round and round over the surface of the waves, sparks and angry flames already spluttering and spurting from the broken engine. Next moment it disappeared beneath the waves in a huge spurt of angry steam.

Below, the deck of the *Cossack* cheered wildly. It was their first kill. But they didn't cheer for long. The first Junker, breaking to port, swept over the ship, dragging its evil black shadow behind it, like a gigantic predatory hawk. Tiny metal eggs tumbled in profusion from its dark blue belly. They grew ever larger. 'Hit the deck!' someone cried, just in time for most of the cheering matelots. Bombs exploded all around the destroyer. It shuddered and heaved as it was blasted from side to side. Hot gleaming silver metal scythed lethally across the deck. Rigging came clattering down. Carley floats exploded as their thin sides were punctured. The bridge house erupted in a plethora of gleaming metal spots, the paintwork steaming and bubbling under the impact, and men who had been whole, hale and hearty a second before lay there stiff and still, never to move again.

Wide Boy shoved the gunner with the false teeth to one side as he hung there dead in his harness. His head lolled hideously to one side, his toothless mouth grinning in one last stupid laugh. Wide Boy flung himself into the firing position. He pressed the trigger. The chicago piano started to chatter frantically. Empty brass cartridges came clattering down to the deck at his feet in a yellow rain. Tracer, white and deadly, sprayed the sky in the path of the starboard Junker. Its bomb doors opened. 'Not tonight, Josephine,' Wide Boy yelled exuberantly, carried away by the unreasoning primeval lust of battle. 'Try this on for fucking size, mate!'

The Junker staggered visibly. It was as if it had just run into an invisible wall. For a moment it appeared to hang there. Small pieces of shredded metal flew from the port engine cowling. At once the prop feathered. The Junker drooped. A red-faced, shrieking Wide Boy could see how the pilot fought desperately to retain control, his face contorted in his leather flying helmet.

For one instant it seemed as if the German pilot was going to do it. But that wasn't to be. Wide Boy let the plane have another tremendous burst. The half-inch bullets ripped the length of the fuselage. The turret splintered into a gleaming spider's web. Blinded, the pilot lost control. The plane came roaring down, trailing thick black smoke behind it. At the very last moment, the pilot managed to heave up the nose to act as a brake and prevent the dying plane from going under.

Then it hit the water. For a moment the plane rested there in a trough. It lay there, belly deep in the water. No sound came from it save that of escaping fuel. The top hatch opened. A lone figure in what appeared to be riding breeches appeared. He threw away his flying helmet, with the radio leads still attached to it. Perhaps he was the upper turret gunner. They never found out. Just as he raised his hands in surrender, there was an angry burst of Tommy gunfire.

'*Scouse!*' Number One yelled from the bridge. Too late. The German crumpled, almost gently, no sound escaping from his suddenly gaping mouth. A line of what seemed like bloody buttonholes was suddenly stitched across his leather flying coat. The next moment he pitched into the water and disappeared for good.

It was about then that the E-boats came surging in and out of the little convoy, weaving back and forth at a tremendous speed, guns chattering to left and right, avoiding collisions at the very last moment, each one of the light wooden German torpedo boats with a huge bone in her teeth.

'Torpedo – port bow!' a lookout yelled frantically.

Number One reacted instinctively as the guns turned their fire on the new attackers who had seemingly appeared from nowhere. 'Hard to starboard!' he screamed. In that same instant he caught the white bubbling trail of the torpedo running just below the surface. The 'fish' was heading straight for the *Cossack*.

The destroyer heeled crazily. Number One held his breath as the captain came running on to the bridge, clad in his shirt and under-pants.

Number One's reaction saved the *Cossack* – that day. As she swung round again just in time, two deadly 'fish', packed with a ton of high explosive, flashed by the ship's bows with only yards to spare. Number One felt his bones turn to water with relief. But there was no time now to dwell on their lucky escape. Four E-boats were hurtling towards the convoy, slamming into each wave as if it were a solid brick wall, their 20mm quick-firers spitting white fire. The tracer shells zipped back and forth in lethal profusion. One of the coastal freighters was hit amidships. It stopped immediately. Fire started to rage at once. Panic-stricken little figures, already alight, blue angry flames searing their bodies, sprang over the side into the icy water – and died there instants later, thrashing madly in their crazy death frenzies.

Vian took over with a quick smile at an emotionally drained Number One, who hung on to the bridge rail as if he would drop if he let go. He rapped out a series of orders with professional ease, hardly seem-ing to notice the flaming carnage to his front, with the convoy splitting up under the E-boat attack, each skipper trying to make his own escape.

The destroyer surged forward, gathering speed by the moment. Her lean, knifelike prow rose out of the water. It sliced through the remains of the downed Junker 88. No one seemed to notice. Wide Boy swung his chicago piano round as an E-boat zipped into the ring sight. He didn't hesitate. He let go a full burst, while Scouse crouched still on the deck among the dead and the smoking debris and watched with unconcealed envy in his angry eyes.

Great chunks of fabric flew from the speeding motor boat. The crooked cross flag was torn to tatters, her bridge shattered. Still she came on. The E-boat and the *Cossack* were now racing towards each other in a collision course. The wounded tensed. They waited fearfully for the impact. If the *Cossack* were holed and they were thrown into the icy water, they wouldn't survive in their condition.

But that wasn't to be. In the very last second, Captain Vian shouted an order. The helmsman answered immediately. The *Cossack* swung to port in a great curved V of wild white water.

The tactic caught the German E-boat skipper completely by surprise. He failed to respond. When he did, it was too late. A great volley of fire erupted the length of the *Cossack*. It hit the E-boat like a terrible punch from a massive fist. She heeled. Her superstructure, already tumbling down in smoking ruined confusion, hit the water. She swung upright once more and, sinking already, stern first, she took another cruel salvo.

Vian didn't wait to see what happened to the crippled dying E-boat. 'That's the stuff to give the troops!' he cried, eyes blazing with excitement and the almost unbearable lust of battle. 'Now then,' he yelled, as if he were addressing the whole crew instead of a shaken, ashen-faced Number One, 'let's show them what we're made of. HERE COMES THE ROYAL NAVY!'

It wasn't a particularly novel phrase, nor was it overly exciting. But at that time, at the height of the 'phoney war', when the beleaguered little island needed the encouragement of victories, it caught on. Naturally the press would front-page it. 'The New Nelson' they described Vian. 'Bold fight against overwhelming odds' they headlined it in the home papers. Thus, in due course, Captain Vian would gain the new daring assignment soon to come, his admiral rings and a reputation for HMS *Cossack* which would last for years to come, long after the last man to serve on her that day was dead.

Two

Wide Boy lounged against the remains of the shattered ship's boat and read the letter with growing apprehension. All around him chippies hammered, dockies hurried back and forth (they were on double overtime) and supply carts pushed by elderly ratings trundled across the jetty bringing up supplies. The buzz was they'd be sailing on the evening tide. There was a flap on and *Cossack*, damaged as she was, had to be patched up the best the repair crews could manage.

Wide Boy, being the wide boy, had made himself scarce immediately the petty officers had announced their duties as the mail had been distributed. He'd grabbed a pail and mop and had gone hurrying across the battle-littered holed deck, crying to no one in particular, 'Make way for a high-ranking officer. Captain's head – blocked. It's an emergency.'

Scouse had watched him go, sneering. 'Yer, that's all that a cockney bastard like

101

you is good for – cleaning out the skipper's shithouse.'

Wide Boy had ignored the comment. He was too eager to read his letter from the girl in Hull, for like most sailors he believed in foresight and such arcane matters and had experienced a growing feeling that this letter to him, completely out of the blue, boded no good.

Now, as he read the awkward pencilled scrawl, he realised he was right. She wrote in a childish hand – but then she was only sixteen – 'I've been to the doctor and he says he's sure – almost. I daren't tell my mum. She'd have a blue fit.'

'Christ Almighty,' Wide Boy muttered to himself, rolling his unlit Woodbine from one end of his mouth to the other in agitation. 'Silly cow, she's gorn and got hersen a bun in the oven. Don't she know nuthin?'

He'd picked her up down Hedon Road, that long street that ran along Hull docks, the time they had sailed in for repair after the 1939 fiasco. It was a rough working-class district, housing dockies and a fair number of amateur tarts who made their money by selling themselves when their fishermen husbands were out at sea with their battered trawlers. It was the usual kind of run-down place that sailors resorted to when they were in a hurry and wanted some fun, the 'four Fs', as they called it – 'find 'em, feel 'em, fuck 'em and forget 'em.'

In the blackout behind the air-raid shelters that smelled of dog piss and puke, he had had his hand up her skirt in no time. She had been a pathetic skinny specimen, with no tits to speak of. But she'd been excited, he'd figured that out almost as soon as he had picked her up and had lightly brushed his hand across her little nipples under her thin dress. She'd bitten him straight off with a delicious moan.

A few minutes later, after a fag (which had set her off coughing as if she'd never smoked before) he'd been all over her, and she hadn't objected. She hadn't even asked for money. So he reasoned she wasn't one of those amateurs who had sent their kids off to sleep with a glass of milk, through which they'd bubbled gas from the kitchen jet, and then gone out on the razzle. 'Gin and it, fish an' tatie supper and Bob's yer frigging uncle.' That kind.

No, she was simply a natural talent: a rare bint that liked to be snaked without asking too many questions and setting too many regulations. A matelot's dream, indeed.

He put his eager, damp, sweating hand on her stocking top. There they usually started playing up. 'What kind of a girl do you think I am? Take yer hand away or I'll scream...'

That kind of bullshit. But she didn't object. Feeling himself harden painfully now, a real frigging diamond-cutter, he had slipped his fingers under the elastic of her tight knickers. Again she hadn't objected.

'Bloody hell,' he had panted to himself, '*she*'s frigging ready for it!'

A few inches more and the tips of his fingers, touching in between that little hairy thing, told him he was right. She wanted it badly. He freed one hand and sought blindly for his contraceptive. Ever since he had had his first experience at his local council school, he had always been careful to carry a french letter. He wanted neither the pox nor to get a girl in the family way: that cost money.

But she couldn't wait. 'Come on ... come on!' she had panted and he had felt her heart beating frantically inside her skinny little ribcage. 'Do it to me ... *please* ... Stick it in ... Your prick.'

The word shocked him. A girl of that age, even on Hedon Road, shouldn't talk to a sailor in that way. But now sex, blind and unreasoning, had taken over. 'But don't you want me to wear something—'

She cut him off, pushing his hand in between her legs. '*Quick* ... *quick*,' she cried, almost as if in despair. 'Oh, I *do* want it!'

That had done it. He had thrown caution

104

to the winds. Still playing with her with one hand, he had undone the flap of his trousers and pulled out his engorged member. 'Stop talking dirty like that,' he choked. 'I'm nearly coming already.'

'Sorry,' she answered. 'I'm sorry.'

But Wide Boy was no longer listening.

He thrust his penis into the girl, nuzzling the source of all pleasure. But it didn't seem to work. While the skinny girl worked her loins back and forth in what seemed a frenzy of sexual lust, he couldn't really penetrate her. 'Hey,' he began.

'Please ... oh please,' she cut in. 'Do it now ... I can't bear it. Don't stop ... oh, please!'

'Bugger this for a lark,' he cursed and thrust with all his strength. She screamed. It was as if she had been stabbed to the death. He felt her freeze, grow stiff and resistant. But he no longer cared about her. He was concentrated solely on his own pleasure. Gripping her skinny buttocks with all his strength so that she couldn't escape him, he thrust once more. Mightily. He felt his penis flood with something hot and sticky. He had no time to consider what it was. He was gasping hard now, head contorted to one side, as if someone were trying to choke him. In and out he thrust his loins, as if he were running some tremendous race, with the girl joining in now. Both clung to the other, biting, kissing, hurting, and then it was over. He felt a massive sense of relief as he collapsed against her and simply slumped there, listening to her heart thud and realising for the first time what that hot and sticky feeling had been. She wasn't a tart at all, but a little kid who had wanted to grow up in a crazy world – fast. She had been a virgin and he had taken her virginity. He felt a sudden sense of elation. This would be one to tell his oppos on the *Cossack*. 'I found a ruddy virgin in Hedon Road, the only one in Hull, mates, and she gave it to me for nuthing—'

The thought died abruptly just as suddenly as it had come. He had pumped her full of his spunk. Christ, if she was daft enough to sacrifice her ring to a sailor whose name she didn't know and whom she'd met only an hour or two before – and not for a penny piece, not even a shandy ... why, she'd be daft enough to go and get frigging pregnant.

Hastily he withdrew from her. She leaned forward in the darkness to stroke the back of his head lovingly. He dodged her. His mind raced electrically. How was he going to get out of this one? If she got in the family way, she'd be pestering him to marry her. Christ Almighty, with so many women about, all panting for it – the war seemed to have made women very randy – he wasn't gonna waste his best years on some skinny teenage tart, whose name he didn't know.

Then help came his way. Over at the Alexandria Docks, there came the first thin wail of a siren. The Jerries were coming for their regular nightly visit to Hull. This was his escape. 'Quick,' he snapped. 'Get inside that shelter ... They'll be over in half a mo.'

'Will you come with me?' There was a note of pleading in her plaintive East Yorkshire voice now, as if she had already half realised that she was going to be betrayed.

'Sorry, love. Got to report to my ship. It's King's Regs.' He shoved his cap on hard and did up his flaps.

'But what's your name?' she called as the wail of the sirens was taken up by others closer at hand.

In the streets behind Hedon Road, the wardens started to shrill their whistles urgently. 'Into the shelters everybody ... Come on, make it sharpish now!'

'Ginger,' he lied glibly.

'Ginger what?'

But by now the guns had opened up. He told himself that was cover enough. 'Got to go!' he yelled as she grabbed at him blindly and he dodged, but as he did so he saw her thin waiflike face, saw it properly for the first time, outlined by the flash of the anti-

aircraft barrage. Wide Boy gasped. Then he
told himself it was due to the surprise of the
guns opening up. Later, in his last few
moments of life on this earth, he knew it
had been because the girl, whose very name
he didn't know then, was so strikingly
beautiful.

Then he was running all out through the
myriad of shabby little nineteenth-century
streets off Hedon Road with the flares
coming down in profusion, followed by the
incendiaries, scattering icy white sparks
everywhere, until he reached the dock gate
and realised for the first time that he had
taken off his gas mask haversack just before
he had fucked her and that the inner khaki
lining had his name, number and ship
written on it in indelible ink for all to see.

And he had left the container at her very
feet...

That had been the start of it. She'd traced
him all right. Now he had the result. She
was in the bleeding family way. He stared
blankly at the pathetic little letter, suddenly
feeling very trapped, that old cockney spirit
which had been bred into generations of his
kind – cocky, smiling, always ready with a
joke and boast – vanished.

It was thus that Number One came across
him while going about his duties, acting the
part of second-in-command well, joking,

ordering, cajoling, playing his official task of being the liaison between the captain and his crew to his full ability. 'Hello, Wilson,' he said, 'you're looking down in the dumps. Face only a mother could love, what?'

Hastily Wide Boy whipped the letter behind him, as if he didn't wish the officer to see it, though there was really no need for him to conceal it. He muttered something about being a bit tired and Number One smiled sympathetically, saying, 'It's that after-action feeling, I shouldn't be surprised. We all feel like that. Anyway, I've got a bit of good news for you.'

'What, sir?' Wide Boy asked without interest; he was far too concerned with the letter and the girl's bad news.

'The captain tried to get you a gong for the recent action. No luck, I'm afraid. Their Lordships are pretty tight with their medals. But we did get you an MID.' He smiled winningly.

'MID?'

'Yes. Mentioned in Dispatches, Wilson. You're the first member of the crew of the *Cossack* to win an award for bravery in this war. Jolly good show. I'm sure you'll write home to your old mum to tell her that.' He nodded. 'Carry on.' Number One went to talk to the next sailor.

'Write to me old mum,' Wide Boy echoed.

'Yer, to tell her she's gonna be a granny at thirty-six. Oh yes, she'll be bleeding proud of her son then ... I don't frigging well think.'

A few moments later, with the letter safely tucked away in his pocket, where it seemed to burn through the cloth to his very flesh, he returned to his duty station only to bump into Scouse. 'Jammy bugger,' the latter sneered through gritted teeth.

Wide Boy stared back at the Liverpudlian in bewilderment while a few of the other ratings on deck reached across to shake his hand and mutter congratulations. Not Scouse, however. He continued with, 'I suppose they have to give awards to somebody – especially those who suck up to the frigging officers. But I'll tell yer this, you cockney arsehole, I could have knocked all them Junkers out of the sky before you'd cocked the weapon.'

Suddenly Wide Boy got it. He snapped out of his blue mood at the letter and said, 'You've had your days as a gunner, mate.' He indicated the broom in the other man's reddened gnarled hands. 'That's what you're good for, mate – pushing a broom around. Try yer best and maybe they'll give you a gong for that – I don't frigging think.'

Scouse clenched a fist like a small steam shovel, suddenly quivering with barely

110

suppressed rage. 'One day, you cocky bugger, I'm gonna plant one on yer ugly kisser that you'll be drinking through yer frigging ribs for a week or two.'

Wide Boy took it in his stride. 'Send me a postcard when you're ready, yer Scouse git.' Gently he pushed his enemy to one side and sauntered past in his best wide-boy style, saying over his shoulder as he did so, 'I say you chappies, I hope I haven't frightened the poor fellow into wetting hissen. If I have, I wonder if you'd be kind enough to change his nappies for him—' He ducked instinctively as Scouse's pail went flying by his head. 'Ta-ta for now...'

Three

They sailed again for Norwegian waters in mid-February. For once they had almost definite sailing orders, though Captain Vian didn't like them. If they were carried out to the letter, he reasoned, Britain might well have to go to war with Norway; and he, for one, didn't want to go down in the history of the Royal Navy as the skipper who took the old country into an unnecessary war.

'If we find her, Number One,' he told his second-in-command in a hushed voice, as they sailed down the length of the fjord and into the open sea that morning, 'I'm going to ask their Lordships for a written instruction. I'm not taking the can for Mr Churchill.'

'Oh, I think things should go all right, sir,' Number One tried to reassure a worried-looking Vian. 'After all, we're not going to get involved in a shooting war, just the rescuing of some of our own chaps.'

Vian wasn't convinced. 'I'm not so sure

about that, Number One,' he said gloomily.

Naturally the crew of the *Cossack* were told nothing of these worries, however. The official buzz was that they were sailing to do an ice reconnaissance of the Skagerrak. But none of the men believed the buzz. They knew that since the *Graf Spee* had sunk itself in the River Plate rather than come out and fight the waiting British ships, the powers that be in Whitehall had been looking for the German *Altmark*, the *Graf Spee*'s supply ship, which had taken aboard all the merchant marine prisoners that the German warship had captured during its short raiding career. 'It's them poor sods, mates, that we're after, mark my words,' they said, 'and they deserve to be rescued from Old Jerry.' And the more imaginative had added, 'And there's gonna be a quid bonus from the Cunard Line for every one of the men we bring back.' At which those reservists who had been called back from their jobs in the great shipping companies had commented mockingly, 'That'll be the frigging day ... that'll be the day!'

Now the small fleet of five destroyers under the command of the cruiser *Aurora* set course due east right into the North Sea before breaking up into single ships to sweep a wide area of the winter sea in pre-determined patterns.

Conditions were rough, both outside and inside the *Cossack*. It was the worst winter in a quarter of a century and the captain had to shorten the watches to prevent the lookouts getting frostbite. Lines had to be rigged too along the deck. They were slick with sheet ice and whenever the weather let up a little, the deck watches were kept busy chipping ice, a back-breaking, freezing task.

Inside the *Cossack* things were even worse. There had been a severe outbreak of flu that winter in the Royal Navy, especially among the 'hostilities only' men. Indeed, the *Cossack* itself had taken aboard some thirty replacements straight from training to make up for crew members who had been hospitalised with the flu germ. But with it the flu had also brought bad cases of what the ratings called 'the squitters', which had them running constantly for the heads, crying, 'Make way ... it's a frigging emergency!' They might well have been cheered on by their laughing mates but the results weren't at all cheering.

Number One, brought up in the spartan but trim, highly polished conditions of the pre-war navy, was appalled by the squalor every morning when he did his rounds of the lower deck – 'home sweet home', as the chief petty officer who guided him would announce cynically. The long naked steel rooms, lit by single naked electric bulbs; the mess table between the lines of hammocks, a wasteland of dirty mugs and tin plates, with the invariable big tin of plum jam with a spoon sticking out of it. Here the men lived, slept and ate. No wonder, he always told himself, trying not to breathe in the stench, the men succumbed so easily to infections, including TB.

But it was the 'ablutions', a line of tin basins scummed with weeks of dirt and hard water, and the heads which always made Number One want to puke there and then. He knew the men had hot water at the ready in a big metal kettle to use in the basins; but invariably when they came off duty, chilled to the bone, they used it to make themselves a quick mug of warming 'char'.

As for the heads, decorated as they were with crude sexual graffiti and the like – 'It's no use standing on the seat, the crabs in this place jump six feet' – they were beyond the pale. And he could stand the place, with its noxious odour and stained chunks of paper torn from the *Daily Mirror* and the like, only for seconds at the most.

As he told the captain on more than one occasion, 'I just don't know how they can stand it, sir. I know most of the HO men are working-class chaps, but even back at home they'd have better facilities than that. Even if they had to use an outside lavatory.'

'I know, I know,' Vian would agree, but Number One could see that his mind was elsewhere. The hunt for the *Altmark* took precedence. The men would simply have to live with these sordid, unworthy conditions the best they could.

On the morning of 14 February, they heard a Norwegian patrol boat had located and stopped the *Altmark*. A Norwegian officer from the craft, the *Trygg*, had requested boarding permission and the chance to search. But, as the Admiralty learned from their own private sources and passed on to Vian, the Norwegian had not got further than the bridge, where the German captain assured him his ship was an unarmed tanker. '*Bribed!*' had been Vian's tight-lipped disappointed comment.

Next day the *Altmark*, now within Norwegian waters, was stopped again by the Norwegian gunboat *Snoegg*, north of the port of Bergen. Again only questions were asked, but no search was undertaken. A little later she was stopped yet again, this time by a Norwegian destroyer, the *Garm*. Her captain himself boarded the *Altmark* with the intention of searching her. The German skipper refused. The Norwegians now ordered the *Altmark* to leave the fortified area of Bergen. Perhaps the Admiralty Intelligence officers under Admiral Godfrey's command guessed the Norwegians suspected the *Altmark* was playing some sort of covert game off Norway, just as the Royal Navy would soon be doing.

But for the time being, Churchill ordered Vian, 'Find her, edge her into the open sea, board her and liberate her prisoners.'

Despite the flu, the squalor and the terrible freezing weather, a great cheer went up from the lower deck when Vian informed them of the news. Even Scouse was seen to give a wary half-smile. But as Wide Boy, the quickest and most intelligent of his mess, said to his shipmates over cocoa and corned beef doorsteps that night, 'If the skipper can't edge the *Altmark* into the open sea, we'll have to stop her in Norwegian waters and that, mateys, could mean a bloody lot of trouble.'

'How do yer mean?' someone asked.

Wide Boy looked at him in the yellow light cast by the single electric bulb. 'War, perhaps.'

It was the same sort of feeling that made Captain Vian uneasy. For the signals office had twice reported to him that day that the airways were full of coded German signals. As he phrased it, 'You'd think, sir, that the whole of the bloody German Navy had sailed from the mouth of the Baltic and was heading for or is already in Norwegian waters. God knows why.'

Vian could have made an educated guess, but he kept his thoughts to himself and concentrated on finding the *Altmark* as ordered by Churchill. Not that that was going to be easy, he knew. There were hundreds of fjords in that part of the world into which she could have slipped and hidden and, as no one had a recognition chart and no clear idea of what the German prison ship looked like, it seemed he would be forced to stop every suspicious merchant ship the *Cossack* encountered and make a search. As Vian cursed in frustration to his Number One, 'This could take all the bloody war!'

Then Vian struck lucky. Two Hudsons of Coastal Command took off from Thornaby in Tess Bay on the morning of Friday the 16th. For a change the weather was glorious, bright and clear and slightly sunny. It was just right for reconnaissance. Splitting up when they reached the Danish coast, the two twin-engined planes started to beat up the Skaggerak as far as Skagen. Suddenly, at twelve that day, the most northerly of the Hudsons radioed that it had spotted a tanker steaming fast in a southern direction. It was a false alarm. But now the Vian group had smelt blood. With tension running high among the crews, the flotilla steamed northwards at full speed, the lookouts falling over each other in the attempt to be first to spot the German ship.

At quarter to three that day they spotted her. Three ships of Vian's flotilla began to steam a parallel course to the German prison ship, while Vian signalled her to steam west, out of Norwegian territorial waters.

The skipper of the *Altmark* was no fool. He knew what the Tommies were after; once out of Norwegian waters they'd board him and free the 400 prisoners he held packed down below in the hold. He started to steer his ship towards the nearest fjord, that of Joessing, where he had already spotted two ancient Norwegian torpedo boats beginning to leave their anchorages and head for the British ships.

Vian knew immediately what the German was up to. 'He's attempting to start an international incident, especially if those two old Norwegian tubs–' he indicated the Norwegian torpedo boats – 'try to stop us.' He paused thoughtfully for a few moments, as the *Altmark* began to disappear into the narrow entrance to the fjord, flanked on both sides by snow-capped barren mountains. 'Number One, I think this is a job for the frocks.'

'Sir?'

'Let Mr Churchill make the decision. He got us into it. He'll have to get us out of it. Call up the radio officer. I want to send an urgent signal to their Lordships.'

Vian's signal caused consternation in London. The War Cabinet had plans of its own for neutral Norway but in the slow timid fashion which had characterised the Chamberlain government ever since the commencement of the war, the politicians who ran Britain didn't want to take any chances. There were suggestions and counter-suggestions. A sizeable minority was for doing nothing. What did the fate of a couple of hundred merchant seamen matter? Most of them were niggers and wogs as it was. But one man held out firmly – obstinately, some of his cabinet colleagues thought – for action. It would be the merchant navy, he opined, who would save the island kingdom from starvation. Those men, whatever their age, race or colour, had to be protected. How otherwise could the country expect them to risk their lives to bring in the food and other supplies the country needed? The rescue of the *Altmark* prisoners would set a signal. It would show the merchant navy that the government was prepared to risk another war to protect them.

Hands tucked into the pockets of his waistcoat, glancing down and around at his colleagues over the tops of the old-fashioned half-glasses he affected, Churchill thundered, as if he were addressing a public meeting at the hustings, 'Gentlemen, we cannot hesitate. We have hesitated long enough, God knows. Our men need us. They need a decision *NOW*!' He paused for dramatic effect and then settled his gaze on Chamberlain's haggard old man's face as if challenging the prime minister personally to say nay.

Chamberlain opened his mouth, almost as if he were going to do just that. Then he remembered his reputation in the House. There were plenty of members who would be only too glad to see the back of him and he knew, too, who would replace him as premier. Winston Churchill! He shut his mouth promptly.

Churchill's eyes blazed with triumph. 'I say go. And you gentlemen?' There was only one answer to that overwhelming question...

Four

'So Max Miller comes on the stage with two sticks and he sez, "This is Hitler's left leg and this 'un here is Hitler's right leg." Course nobody knows what he's going on about. But he's the cheeky chap and they're all laughing their heads off and rolling in the aisle, and then he goes back o' the stage and comes out agen with two great big taties – huge things – and he's carrying them bent down in his crotch. By now they're all rolling in the aisles cos they think he's gonna say these is Hitler's bollocks. But yer know Max Miller. He looks at some Judy in the audience and he sez, with that dead cheeky look of his, "No, missus, you've got it wrong ... dead wrong. These is King Edwards".'

The raconteur paused as if he expected a burst of laughter, a comment, anything. But nothing came. The boarding party was too tense as they crouched there at the bows of the *Cossack* advancing into the darkening fjord at a snail's pace, every gun directed at the stark outline of the *Altmark*, only half a mile ahead.

Number One, in charge of one of the two sections, stared to his front, cast in the silver spectral light of a full moon. Beyond the *Altmark* was a small town of some kind perched on the top of sheer cliffs at least a thousand feet high. The place seemed, as far as he could make out, to consist of a factory, what looked like a sawmill with a tall chimney, and a huddle of wooden houses. But did it contain Norwegian soldiers? he wondered as they crept ever closer to their objective. If it did and it came to an exchange of fire, the boarding parties, armed only with clubs, bayonets and handfire weapons, wouldn't stand much of a chance against soldiers who probably had machine guns. Number One said a quick prayer that there were no squaddies up there. They sailed on, the only sound their own heavy breathing and the steady beat of the *Cossack*'s engines. It wouldn't be long now.

On the bridge, directing the operation, Vian knew he had tried everything in his power to avoid such a confrontation, which might cause a war between Britain and Norway. He had conveyed the gist of Churchill's order to the Norwegian authorities but they had refused to play ball. Indeed, they had hindered his flotilla, and, he guessed for some reason known to themselves – perhaps it was the sale of their precious Narvik iron ore that was blinding them to reality – they were siding with the Huns.

Not that it mattered much now. The die was cast. An hour before he had assembled the crew and addressing the boarding party specifically, he had announced in that crisp, no-nonsense old-style naval fashion of his, 'We've got to get those prisoners off. They're our chaps and come hell or high water, men, they're coming home with us. Got it?'

Standing in front of the men, already dressed in his seaboots and with a revolver at his waist, Number One had wondered for a moment whether he should call on the crew for three cheers. Then he had thought better of it. It would be wiser to leave the cheering till they'd got the *Altmark*'s prisoners off the prison ship; there was many a slip between the cup and the lip.

Now all that was history. War or not, they were going in, and Number One guessed that the Norwegian naval authorities had tipped off the Huns that they were on their way. Suddenly he wondered if he should have brought the traditional boarding cutlass, for he guessed there was going to be trouble, and plenty of it.

For Scouse, crouched just behind the officer and smelling strongly of rum, stolen under threats from the newcomers on board, the prospect of trouble was highly exciting. As he slapped one gloved fist against the other with a strange metallic sound, he muttered, 'Any frigging Jerry trying to stop Mrs O'Leary's handsome son is in for a frigging surprise. He'll be missing a set of teeth right smartish.' He chuckled in that malicious manner of his at the thought of his illegal brass knuckles smashing into some German's face and turning it into a toothless, bloody mess.

Now the *Cossack* was nosing its way through the crackling surface ice at about five knots, every man tense with excitement, the boarding parties leaning forward as if they were being buffeted by a strong wind. Ahead the great bulk of the *Altmark*, all twelve thousand tons of her, loomed larger and larger. Vian, on the bridge, made his calculations. The boarding party would have to be pretty nimble. There was a distance, he estimated, of eight feet between the *Cossack*'s forecastle head and the *Altmark*'s quarterdeck. Any one of the boarding party who missed his footing didn't stand a chance. He'd be either crushed to death or frozen and drowned in the icy waters of the fjord. Frowning a little, Vian bent and

ordered, 'Engine room ... Dead slow both!'
The *Cossack* started to come to a halt.

Suddenly – startlingly – the icy beam of a
searchlight stabbed the silver gloom. It hit
Vian directly in the face. He threw up his
arm to shield his eyes. The bridge party did
the same, momentarily blinded by that
sudden light from the *Altmark*. 'Tricky Hun
bugg—' Captain Vian cursed as in the same
instant the German prison ship lunged
astern of the almost motionless destroyer.
Vian reacted the best he could. He bellowed
an order at the equally blinded helmsman
and swung the destroyer about. But it was
too late. The *Altmark* scraped the length of
the *Cossack* with a nasty rending noise of
damaged, tearing metal.

'NOW!' Number One yelled, realising that
the balloon had gone up; the damned German ship was about to attempt to escape yet
once again.

'No, Jimmy the One—' Vian cried. Too
late.

The young second-in-command drew a
last great breath. Next moment he launched
himself into space. He didn't dare look
down at that patch of thin ice so far below.
If he missed his hold, he'd fall and go
through. More than likely, he'd be ground
to a bloody pulp by the action of the two
ships.

Number One slammed into the side of *Altmark*. The upper metal was sheer black ice. Blindly, gasping as if he were running a great race, he grabbed for a hold. Something sharp ripped off his middle fingernail. He yelped. A blinding electrical pain had shot up his right hand. But he had to hold on – and he did.

Now they were following Number One's daring leap into the unknown. A rating slipped and disappeared between the two ships with a piercing scream that would haunt the others for the rest of their short lives. Below he was ground to a bloody paste, as the *Altmark* reversed her powerful engines, her screws churning the water into a white bubbling frenzy.

'She's trying something else,' Vian cried urgently as the *Altmark* moved back. 'Watch the bugger ... she's capable of anyth—'

Next moment the *Altmark* raced forward again to ram the much smaller destroyer. But the German ship was out of luck. Coming at the *Cossack* stern first, a daring manoeuvre at night, her skipper hadn't reckoned with the quickness of the well-trained Royal Navy bridge crew. Just when it seemed the great bulk of the German ship would smash into the *Cossack* and hurl her, holed and sinking, on to the cruel rocks only yards away, the helmsman spun his wheel round.

127

The *Cossack* heeled and shuddered dramatically. But despite the fact she was almost motionless, she answered to the wheel. She turned. In that same instant, the stern of the *Altmark* struck the rocks. Next instant she was stuck there fast and for the first time, her defenders, hidden so far, but knowing now that they were in a fix, rose above the side and began popping off angry shots at the advancing boarding party.

They didn't wait for an order to react. Number One, recovered from his near fall, but panting hard, raised his .38. He pressed the trigger. The big service revolver jerked. For a moment he thought he had missed. But his target, a German officer firing his pistol from the bridge of the *Altmark*, groaned suddenly. It was almost a sad sound, as if he were feeling sorry for himself for being hit like this. His knees buckled. His revolver clattered to the deck from abruptly nerveless fingers. Next moment he dropped after it and lay still, dead or unconscious, Number One neither knew nor cared. For the first time in his service career, he was animated by the fierce joy of battle. 'Come on, lads,' he cried. 'In and at 'em!'

They needed no urging. They surged forward over the well deck. Firing and shrieking they started to push the German

128

defenders back. Then a German rose from behind a gantry, right in Scouse's path. He held some sort of knife or short cutlass in his right hand. He yelled, 'Stirb ... Englander!'

The Liverpudlian knew not what he said. But he did know that the German merchant seaman wasn't 'gonna offer me a cup of China tea with warm milk,' as he told his admiring shipmates later. 'So I clocked him.' He did indeed. Those cruel brass knuckles flashed in the light of the searchlights. The blow caught the German right in the centre of his face. His nose was squashed. Blood shot everywhere. He reeled back, spitting blood and teeth, which shone like polished ivory in that crimson gore.

Scouse laughed. As he paused to spring over the groaning German, he seemed to be seized by an afterthought. With all his strength he kicked the German in the groin. The wounded man screamed: a scream that was cut short by the hot vomit which suddenly flooded his throat. His hand flew to his ruined testicles. Next moment his head lolled to one side like that of a broken doll and he was unconscious or dead.

Here and there the Germans were beginning to surrender. Dropping their weapons and raising their arms, they started to cry, 'Kamerad.' It had no effect on Scouse. 'I'll give yer frigging "kamerad",' he chortled, cruelly punching and kicking those who surrendered until the second-in-command yelled harshly, 'None of that. Treat them with respect, you bloody big oaf.'

Grumbling, Scouse let go of the unfortunate German cook, whose face he was 'polishing', as he phrased it, with his knuckledusters.

Here and there, however, individual Germans still fired back until Number One, summoning up his best German, cried, 'Nicht mehr scheissen. Genug.' What he had said in actual fact was 'no more shitting'. But it had the desired effect.

The firing began to ebb away. The Germans dropped their weapons. Suddenly doors were opened everywhere, and grey-faced men of every age and colour came tottering towards their rescuers, crying wildly, 'We've been saved!'

Number One heard himself echoing that somewhat trite phrase that would be on the headlines of every British newspaper soon and would go down resounding through the years to come: 'THE NAVY'S HERE!'

Five

'Did you see how they waved and cheered?' they enthused. 'Christ, they thought we was real heroes!'

'Won't get me no more free beer,' they moaned. 'Holy cow, my plates o' meat is killing me. I didn't join the Royal to do no marching!'

'They say we're gonna be on Pathé News,' they said. 'I saw the camera bloke with his cap back to front on top of their van near the town hall as we did the eyes right.'

'Come off it, matey,' they jeered. 'All they'll show is the frigging officers and gents with their medals and swords. Blokes like us ordinary matelots ain't got a frigging look-in.'

'Aye, that's right,' they agreed with a note of pride, 'but you must admit, the crowds did us proud – and I tell yer this, mates, anyone of this here old *Cossack* who's sharp off the mark this evening'll get his oats for free. Even yon hero, Scouse.'

As expected of him, Scouse pulled a fierce

face and doubled his hamlike fist threaten-ingly. All the same, he was pleased that Number One had recommended him for a gong for his bravery in the *Altmark* boarding action. If he got it, it'd be one in the frigging eye for that cockney tosspot, Wide Boy.

At that moment, his rifle on his bunk, the white from the blancoed equipment still powdering his best blues, Wide Boy was staring at the letter among the other mail which the postal clerk had placed on the divisional mess table while they'd been on the celebration parade in Newcastle. He knew it was from her; there was no mistaking that childish pencilled scrawl. He slapped the blanco off his jersey and put out a hand to pick up the pregnant girl's letter to him, then stayed his hand in mid-air. Why spoil things?

One of the happy sailors, now released from the constraints of the parade under the hawk eyes of the petty officers, was saying, 'Did you see that Judy with the big tits in the front row as we did the eyes right? God, did she have bumpers! I bet a bloke could get his head in between them and know no pain for twenty-four hours at least.'

'What kind of nancy boy or pervert are you, Chalky? Get yer head between her bumpers? I'd rather get me hampton in between summat else. Wouldn't you, lads?'

There was an outburst of happy agreement from the young sailors as they prepared themselves for the brief shore leave.

Wide Boy let his hand drop. He'd read the letter later. Anyway, he knew what it would contain. More bloody moans and threats and 'what me mum sez' rubbish. He wanted to enjoy himself in Newcastle. After what had happened in the fjord when they had tackled the *Altmark*, he realised that even in the *Cossack* he might well be croaked at any time. Why worry about the future? Let it look after itself. *He* had to live for the day. 'At what time's the liberty boat, mates?' he cried with sudden renewed enthusiasm. He pulled out his metal shaving mirror and looked at himself as if he couldn't quite believe that anyone could be that handsome, while the others blew him wet noisy kisses and gave faint cries as if in the throes of extreme dying passion. 'I can't disappoint them Judies out there, yer know.'

'Fuck you,' Scouse said with his usual lightning wit, but no one was listening to the new 'hero' now. Their minds were abruptly intent on women, the night and the adventures that might befall them in the blacked-out streets of the northern city. Abruptly life seemed very exciting.

On the other side of the North Sea Grossadmiral Raeder, head of the German Navy, had plans for the men of the *Cossack*. In effect, his plans would ensure that they had excitement and adventure in plenty. But not with the 'bints and boozers' of working-class Newcastle.

The aged head of the German Navy, with his old-fashioned stiff wing collar and haughty manner, which cut him off from the younger officers at the great final conference, looked round the crowded operations room and said simply: 'Meine Herren, the Führer in his great wisdom has made his decision. We invade Norway.' He raised his weak hand to stop the expected roar of surprise. 'It is a decision about which the Führer has thought a great deal. But now it is clear that our arch enemy Churchill–' he pronounced it 'Schurschill' – 'is urging the English premier to do the same, it is imperative that we beat the Tommies into Norway.' He paused and let his announcement sink in.

Many of the senior officers of the Kriegsmarine present knew that this meant that the Reich was invading a neutral country for the second time. But they knew too that the reputation of the German Navy was at stake. The Führer thought little of the navy; indeed, he avoided going to sea altogether if possible and was often seasick while still in harbour. If things turned out wrongly, he'd abandon the navy in favour of the army and air force. The navy had to prove itself, and a maritime operation like an invasion of Norway would allow them to show Hitler what their ships could do.

Raeder seemed to read his senior officers' thoughts, for he said, 'We shall of course do our utmost to make this operation successful. But remember, we are fighting the greatest navy in the world, the English Royal Navy. Indeed, we cannot match the Tommies ship for ship.' He paused and lowered his voice in the manner of a professional orator so that his audience had to come in closer and strain to hear his words. 'But the English have a weakness. Their naval air force is antiquated. No match for ours. So the only real cover their capital ships have is their destroyers – and in the light of all their commitments, the English don't have too many of those. So, gentlemen, once the operation starts, our primary duty apart from conveying the army to Norway is to obliterate as many of their destroyers as possible – and quickly!'

Here and there senior officers nodded their agreement. The Royal Navy, they knew, had been starved of funds by the English government for years. As a consequence, its capital ships were antiquated, had poor armour and anti-aircraft devices. They'd be no match for the Stuka dive-bombing squadrons of the Luftwaffe. Thus, without the protection of the fast-moving English destroyers, they'd be too vulnerable to be risked out in the open sea; they'd have to stick to the safety of their great anchorage at Scapa Flow. Without the capital ships, the English would not be able to stop German cruisers, all built since 1934, from landing troops in the Norwegian ports.

'So, as you can readily understand, the eradication of the English destroyer fleet is a prerequisite for the success of this operation,' Raeder continued. For the first time emotion showed in the old Grand Admiral's wrinkled, severe face. 'In particular we must knock out the fastest and most modern of the English destroyer fleet – those of the Tribal Class. We all know what trouble they have caused us quite recently with the *Altmark*. They must be liquidated!'

There was a murmur of approval from both the old and young officers. The way the English had cocked a snook at the Norwegians and had simply liberated their prisoners from the *Altmark* had just added to the disgrace of Captain Langsdorff's suicide and sinking of the *Graf Spee* in the River Plate without any attempt to put up a fight.

'It is a minor matter, I know, gentlemen,' Admiral Raeder continued. 'But if we have a chance, let us make sure that we do it.' He stared hard at the circle of eager young faces, men who would face the supreme test soon: their first action of the war. 'Do what, you ask? I shall tell you. Let us sink that damned *Cossack* and with it, her triple-damned captain, Herr Kapitan Vian!' Raeder stamped his foot down hard.

It was the agreed-upon signal. As if by magic the doors to the great operations room were flung open. Immediately white-jacketed and white-gloved mess stewards swarmed in, bearing silver trays. On them there were glasses, all iced, of schnapps. At once they circulated among the officers, handing out the drinks, while Admiral Raeder, smiling somewhat woodenly, waited.

Finally everyone had a drink. Raeder raised his glass. 'Kameraden,' he declared. At once, as naval etiquette demanded, they raised their glasses in unison till they were parallel with the button of their right tunic pocket.

Raeder cried in his reedy voice, 'To the success of our operation and death to the *Cossack*!'

'To the success of our operation and death to the *Cossack*!' they echoed in a deep bass tone.

As one they drained their glasses and, without a further command, flung them at the great open fireplace, where they shattered like so many exploding bullets as naval custom demanded.

Raeder's old face cracked into a smile. He told himself that, after a naval career full of humiliation and insults – the defeat of the First War, the mutiny of the German Fleet, the forced Allied disarmament, the disgrace of the *Graf Spee* – the Kriegsmarine was going to have its revenge at last...

As drunk as he was, Wide Boy was going to take his revenge, too. The pregnant Judy in Hull with her demands and threats was spoiling his life, as women always did if you were fool enough to fall into their clutches. Now, with this tipsy bird, smelling of cheap Soir de Paris, her knickers already torn off in the pub, ready for it and yet not ready with her silly protestations, he was going to pay her back. He had waited long enough to snake her. Now he was going to stand no more old buck.

But the married woman – her old man was a cook on the *Rodney* in the Med – wasn't in so much of a rush for 'a little bit of the other' out in the cold night at the back of the Cock and Bottle. She kissed passionately, her tongue halfway down his throat, all right, but every time he attempted to push her dress up to reveal her naked loins beneath, she thrust him away, saying in a thick, slurred voice, 'Now then, sailor, don't be in such a hurry. We can allus have a go tomorrow, hinny.'

'No we fucking can't,' he snapped. 'You know the Royal. I could be on my way to Scapa Flow with only the sheep to fuck at six sharp tomorrow morning. Now then, spread them legs and let the dog have a look at the cat.' He rubbed her big loose breasts, her nipples standing out erect in the cold.

In the end, she said, 'All right ... all right, give a lass a bit o' peace. I don't fancy it no more and you're not going to poke me against this wall in this weather, hinny. But I'll ease you off like, if you want to.'

'Ease me off?' he echoed.

'You know,' she said, seemingly suddenly embarrassed. She made an obscene gesture with her clenched hand.

'You mean – gimme a wank?'

'Better than nothing.'

'But I can't go to sea agen on a wank, girl. That's not much to remember you by,' he said incredulously.

'Listen,' she said, 'I know you sailors. You come back from the sea, full o' piss and vinegar. You're drunk, you don't care. You've got more spunk than you know what to do with. And the result – the woman got another bairn in another nine months. No thank you. Besides,' she sniffed, 'I'm a married woman with an allowance from me husband in the *Rodney*.'

'Yer, I know about the frigging *Rodney*.' He cut her short, his good mood vanishing as he thought about the letter waiting for him back on the mess-deck table. It was typical of a woman. Men were happy, wanted a bit of fun and the women played 'em along for so long, but in the end with the Judies, it was allus frigging kids, allowances and roofs over their heads. 'All right.' He gave in. 'Grab a hold of it if you want to.'

She spat delicately into her right hand and took a hold of his distended organ. 'By, you're a big lad, ain't yer?' she said encouragingly. But the compliment didn't work; his good mood had vanished. All he wanted now was to get the heavy water off his chest and head off to the nearest off-licence, where with a bit of luck he might get a half-bottle of spirits and drink himself into oblivion in his bunk on the ship.

She sweated hard until finally he started to groan with pleasure in spite of his mood. Even then she couldn't leave off, however, saying, 'Now watch it. Don't get it all over my dress. It's the one I wear to go dan—'

Too late. He almost collapsed into her arms and pushing his deadweight away, she snapped, 'Oh, you men are dirty, careless buggers, aren't yer just!'

That then was the end of the famous *Altmark* affair, with that famous rallying cry, 'THE NAVY'S HERE', that went around the so-called 'free world' for a couple of days or so. The 'heroes' were soon forgotten and as Wide Boy and the rest of them returned through the darkness to the *Cossack*, some drunk and singing, some sombre and apprehensive for reasons known only to themselves, a few resigned to their fate and blind to their surroundings, as if they were drunker than the rest of their shipmates, the 'free world' abandoned them to what was to come.

Six

Now things moved fast.

On Tuesday 8 April 1940, the Germans marched into neighbouring Denmark. It was all over in half a day. On that same day, German paratroopers started to land in Norway and at the same time a small fleet of German cruisers caught both the Norwegians and the British – who had been proposing an invasion of that neutral country, too – by complete surprise. But unlike their Nordic neighbours, the Danes, the Norwegians began to resist. Even the Norwegian king and royal family decided to flee and fight. But the Germans had powerful friends among the Norwegians. Vidkun Quisling, a Norwegian Nazi, formed a 'Norwegian National Government' with German approval, and the country was divided. That night at eight thirty, the British and French governments declared they would give all possible aid to Norway. Ponderously, the two Allied powers began to prepare to invade Norway.

First into action was the Royal Navy. The German cruisers were sitting ducks as far as the British capital ships were concerned. Trapped at anchorage, unloading troops or between the sea and Norwegian coastal waters, the lighter German ships were easy targets. The Great War battlecruiser the *Renown* scored several severe hits on the most modern but lighter enemy battlecruiser the *Scharnhorst* and she was forced to flee under the cover of a smokescreen. Then the *Renown* set about slaughtering the German's escort ships, sending most of them to the bottom of the sea.

On the following Thursday, five British destroyers under the command of a Captain Warburton-Lee, who would be a hero – and dead – before that day was out, sailed into the Norwegian fjord leading to the iron-ore port of Narvik. Warburton-Lee already knew that the port harboured at least six German destroyers – and all were more modern and more powerful than his own craft. But orders were orders and he sailed on, knowing what to expect.

Just after dawn the one-sided battle commenced. Sailing line abreast, the British craft soon spotted the German destroyers waiting for them, mixed up with plenty of enemy merchant shipping. Before the Germans could react, the five British destroyers opened up with their 'tin fish'. At that range they could hardly miss.

Two German destroyers were hit by the torpedoes straight away. One was torn apart; the other started to flame and sink. The merchantmen started to be hit and burn too. The flames from a whaling ship, caught amidships and full of whale oil, flared high into the dawn sky, illuminating two other German destroyers hiding closer to shore. A German battery opened just then. It didn't stop Warburton-Lee's craft. They closed on the two Germans. The First Battle of Narvik, as it was later called, was in full swing.

Now the Germans began reacting furiously. From a distance of 3,000 yards, three enemy destroyers tackled Warburton-Lee's little force. At first they shot wide, but not for long. Soon they started achieving direct hits on the British. A shell shattered the bridge of HMS *Hardy*, Warburton-Lee's ship, and he and most of his officers were badly wounded. The *Hardy* fought on. HMS *Hunter* went under, riddled and burning. Under the command of the sole remaining officer, Warburton-Lee's naval secretary, the *Hardy* was run aground. The dying captain gave his last command, 'Abandon ship!' He naturally would stay with her. As he died, he called weakly,

'Every man for himself ... good luck!' Then his head lolled to one side.

The First Battle of Narvik had become a British victory. Warburton-Lee won the VC posthumously. He and his crews had done a splendid job. At the cost of two British destroyers sunk and one damaged, they had annihilated two German destroyers, damaged five badly and sunk seven German merchant ships. Now the Germans were bottled up in Narvik, with their mountain troops, who had been holding the place, fleeing into the hills behind the fjord. Narvik was now open for the taking.

Now the *Cossack* was called back to action. She was to act as one of the escorts to the 30,000-ton Great War battleship, the *Warspite*. The task force was to steam into German-held Narvik. There were still eight German destroyers and six merchant ships anchored there, and they could threaten the Franco-British army landing force which was due to arrive soon to help the hard-pressed Norwegian army, now fighting for its very existence. The Germans had to be destroyed ruthlessly and Churchill was prepared to risk the old battleship in those tight, dangerous waters to carry out that task.

The plan was dangerously brutal in its

hurried simplicity. While the destroyers would race at full speed along both sides of the Narvik fjord, tackling primarily the German destroyers but also the coastal batteries if they opened up on the British ships, the *Warspite* would enter more carefully and way off the coastal banks. The battleship would fire over the tops of the destroyer escort, taking out battery after battery and other German emplacements so that they could pose no threat to the Anglo-French land force. It was all very rough and ready, but Churchill reasoned that the *Warspite*'s 'bricks', as her great 15-inch shells were called by the Royal Navy, would do the job of destroying the German defences more speedily than any planned operation drawn up by a bunch of slow, traditional staff officers. As always, the First Lord of the Admiralty had little time for the 'Red-Tab' army staff officers.

Naturally the men of the *Cossack* knew nothing of all this. They did know, however, that they were going to finish off the job started by the H class destroyers under Warburton-Lee, and boasted to anyone who would listen, 'In the end, mate, they allus need the old Tribals, especially the *Cossack*, to make a proper job of it, don't they?'

This time, however, *Cossack* was not going to make such 'a proper job of it' as her cocky crew thought. Indeed, this April, as the destroyer prepared for its second real piece of wartime action, it seemed HMS *Cossack's* luck was beginning to turn – for the worse.

But that April morning, as the *Cossack* set sail again for those northern waters, the crew was light-hearted and full of confidence. After all, they were the fêted 'heroes of the *Altmark*'. Even Scouse seemed in good spirits as he squatted cleaning the firing-pin mechanism of one of the 4.7 inchers, to which he had now returned on Number One's recommendation, his past 'crime' forgotten. Over and over again he was singing the monotonous idiotic chorus of that song which Gracie Fields had made famous that spring.

'She's the girl that makes the thing
That drills the hole that holds the spring
That drives the rod that turns the knob
That works the thingamabob...
That's gonna win the war...'

Over and over again the words were repeated until the others of his turret were so bored that they risked the hot-tempered Liverpudlian's wrath and cried, 'Come on, Scouse, put a frigging sock in it.' To which a happy Scouse merely raised two spread fingers by way of a reply and continued his chant.

Wide Boy, for his part, was happy again, too. He was going to sea. There'd be danger ahead, he knew that, but there'd be adventure as well and he'd be able to forget the threat of lifelong domesticity and boredom that a forced marriage would bring. Besides, there was something else, which he had so far been unable to interpret fully. He had been brought up to be a loner: the cockney spiv who knew the price of everything and the value of nothing. His shallow world had been that of dog eat dog where every man had to look out for himself – or else!

Now his attitude was beginning to change. He was starting to feel that he belonged to a bigger entity than just himself. That April, when perhaps he had just a mere year to live, he had begun to feel that he wasn't so much of a loner after all. There was the ship – 'the good old frigging *Cossack*', as he expressed it to his mates – and his shipmates themselves – 'a bloody bunch of losers, if I do say so, mates, but good lads in their way, even if they couldn't find their way into a knocking shop with a fiver stuck on their foreheads and their John Thomas waving in the wind'. One word said by some matelot about the *Cossack* in a public bar, however, and, like the rest, Wide Boy would snarl threateningly, 'Say that agen, mate, and you'll be lacking a set of front teeth – right smartish!' Indeed, there were some of his more perceptive shipmates who were now predicting, 'Yon cockney bigmouth is gonna be a navy lifer one of these days, you mark my words.'

Now, as the *Cossack* started to catch up with the long, heavy shape of the *Warspite* and her attendant craft, Leading Seaman Wilson could not quite control the heady feeling of excitement that overcame him at the sight. Indeed, it made him shudder with an almost sexual thrill. The good old *Cossack* was sailing into action again. Beyond that grey-purple horizon to the east there was unknown trouble waiting for him and every man on board the destroyer. Each of the *Cossack*'s matelots would be confronted by his personal destiny. But in the final analysis, they'd all be in it together, shipmates one and all, even that bugger Scouse.

Behind him, as the lean destroyer gathered speed, her wake being whipped into a frothy white cream, the coast of England began to disappear into the haze. Ahead lay the green, heaving sea and unknown danger. Standing on the bridge, Number One felt some of the apprehension, yet exhilaration too, experienced by the young HO able seaman. He knew as an officer, second-in-

149

command of one of His Majesty's ships, he should not give way to his imagination. Relatively senior officers – of whom he was one – were supposed to be calm, realistic and objective at all times, especially when they were going into battle as he was. All the same, Number One experienced a strange feeling of unreality; perhaps timelessness was a better word.

Before him generations of other young officers had done exactly what he was about to do. They had gone to war, wondering what the outcome of the battle would be. Would they survive? Would they die? They must have all felt that same sensation of limbo; that unreal quality before it all started and an officer had no further time for reflection on life and the purpose of life.

Suddenly he chuckled. 'Stupid twerp,' he whispered to himself, with an abrupt grin on his handsome young face, 'you'll be waffling *Henry V* soon ... St Crispin's Day and all that twaddle.'

The helmsman looked at him out of the corner of his eyes from his position at *Cossack*'s wheel. 'Poor sod,' he said to himself, 'it's the nervous strain. Young Number One's gone crackers!'

Perhaps he had.

Seven

The lone star shell hissed into the grey sky above the entrance to the fjord. It exploded with a sharp crack. Instantly everything was illuminated in its cruel silver light. It was as if a signal had been lit. Almost at once, a myriad angry cherry-red lights began to ripple along the length of the cliffs to starboard. Next moment the air was full of the harsh hiss of shells. It was like the sound of a great sheet of canvas being ripped apart by some giant hands. An instant later, shells started to plummet down all around the attack force. In a flash the calm dark waters of the fjord were transformed into a mad maelstrom, as water was whipped up everywhere and the cliffs on both sides echoed and re-echoed with the hollow boom of cannonfire. The Second Battle of Narvik had commenced.

Vian broadcast his order to the flotilla. It wasn't needed. His destroyer captains and their officers knew exactly what to do. Indeed, many of them had been waiting and preparing for this moment ever since they had entered Dartmouth as callow boys decades before. The destroyers split up. Each was intent on finding its own prey. Like greyhounds let off the lead, they darted forward, spitting fire, dodging the torpedoes speeding towards them from the land-based torpedo batteries. On the *Cossack* fire orders were rapped out with metallic severity over the tannoy system. 'Bearing green three–oh ... range one thousand yards ... deflection zero ... FIRE!'

In A turret, Scouse yelled with excitement. He was back in his old position at last. 'Try this on for frigging collar size, mate!' he cried, pulling the firing bar. The gun boomed. The extractor whirled madly. The boat rocked and the first salvo of *Cossack*'s Narvik battle went hurtling towards the German destroyer, *Dieter van Roeder*, some thousand-odd yards away where she was lying near the jetty.

'Spot on, Scousey,' one of the loaders yelled exuberantly as the German destroyer rocked and immediately a thick mushroom of black smoke rushed into the sky.

Now everywhere the *Cossack*'s gunners were opening up at this tempting stationary target, seemingly ignoring the fire coming their way from the German land-based batteries. Disregarding the shells falling all around the lean grey destroyer as she drew ever closer to her German opponent, they opened up everywhere with a resounding crash like the dramatic start of some primeval Wagnerian overture. Their new Oerlikon cannon from Switzerland chattered crazily. A steady stream of white-glowing 20mm shells hissed slickly over the intervening distance, bouncing off the German destroyer's thicker armour plate like glowing golf balls. Gleaming, steaming yellow cartridge cases tumbled to the deck at the gunners' feet in crazy profusion. Great spouts of crazy white water hurtled into the air on all sides.

Wide Boy, once again behind the chicago piano, those banked rows of heavy machine guns, firing all out so that the very air seemed torn apart by the vicious fury of their ear-shattering noise, could see that the German ship was not only absorbing a terrible punishment from the *Cossack*, but that she was inflicting one, too.

Behind him he had just heard a gantry come tumbling down. On his side of the ship, the Carley floats and lifeboats were already ripped to shreds. Great gleaming metallic scars ripped by the German shells had appeared as if by magic along the whole length of the *Cossack*'s superstructure. 'Come on,' he cursed madly to himself, 'sink the Jerry bastard.' He felt himself suddenly trembling with an unreasoning rage. Why didn't the fucking *Cossack* turret gunners knock her out? For if they didn't soon, the *Cossack* would continue on her present course – one that could only lead to the destroyer's own destruction.

On the shattered bridge, standing in the midst of the smoking debris, Number One felt the same inward anger. As always these modern Hun ships were better and more stoutly built than their British equivalents, constructed in the parsimonious thirties, when governments had won votes by building on the cheap but – naturally – risked the lives of future naval crews. He struck the bulkhead with his fist and raged, 'Come on ... come on, Guns ... Sink the bugger ... *now*!'

But Guns couldn't. That was obvious. The *Dieter van Roeder* was still firing back valiantly and a furious Number One could just make out from the corner of his eye, through the fog of war, that the *Eskimo* had come limping to a stop, the whole front of her bows blown off by shellfire or a torpedo. Instinctively he knew that was going to be the fate of HMS *Cossack*, if they didn't pull an ace out of the pack pretty damned quick. He raised his glasses once again in the very same instant that a German five-inch shell slammed into the *Cossack*'s port side.

The ship quivered and trembled like a live thing which had been badly hurt. There was the shrill scream of rending metal. Smoke, tinged with oil and cherry-red flame, shot upwards. The *Cossack*'s speed suddenly decreased rapidly.

Down on the deck, manning his banks of hammering machine guns, Wide Boy knew the *Cossack* had been hurt – badly. He heard the steam escaping with a tremendous hiss and the screams of the scalded engine-room men as one of her boilers was hit. 'Fuck ... fuck ... *fuck*,' he cursed madly as he tried plunging fire on a German field gun just behind the jetty where the enemy destroyer stood, for he guessed the round which had slammed into the *Cossack* had come from it. And there would be more. For now the *Cossack* was not responding properly to the helm. Her steering gear had been struck and she was drifting, slowly and inevitably, to a land feature which to the ex-cockney barrow boy was known as 'Hankins' Point', why he didn't know nor care at that particular moment. They were in trouble – very serious trouble indeed.

But luck was helping the wounded ship a little. Carried away by rage, Scouse planted a salvo from A turret directly on the crippled German destroyer, shrouded so much by smoke that it was hard to direct fire accurately. Indeed, the only indication that sweating, swearing Liverpudlian had that he had scored a direct hit was the fact that two-hundred-foot gashes of angry scarlet split the murk of battle above her and shot into the sky. Next moment, as the weary gun crew burst into cheering, the *Dieter van Roeder* ceased firing. It was the greatest triumph of Scouse's short naval career and those few who would survive into old age would tell each other over their half-pints at the RNA club, 'Aye, it was that big-mouthed Scouse git who did it ... He saved the *Cossack* back at Narvik in '40.' Not that anyone paid much attention to the aged survivors. Who had ever heard of the Battle of Narvik in the first place, anyway?

Five minutes later it happened. With a resounding crash that jarred every plate and sent men reeling all over the battle-littered smoking deck, the *Cossack* smashed into the rocks just beyond the now silent *Dieter van Roeder*. She came to rest there, free from enemy fire for a moment. But only for a moment. The German alpine infantry of General Dietl's 1st Gebirgsjagerdivision, which had retreated up the heights under the fire of the *Warspite*, now took up the challenge.

In the same instant that the bridge

telegraphs started to signal the alarm, Wide Boy felt a sudden sharp stabbing pain in his upper thigh. It was as if someone had just thrust a red-hot poker into the soft flesh of his left leg. He yelped with the almost unbearable pain of the wound. 'Help me,' he cried thinly. 'I've been hit ... help!'

No one was listening. Everyone had been caught by surprise by the sudden turn of events and, with the German infantry in their peaked caps, adorned with the Edelweiss badge of the elite Alpine Corps, already coming out of their hiding places, firing from the hip as they did so, was too concerned with getting the ship off the rocks before it was too late.

The first to react was, in the end, Number One. The captain had taken over control of the bridge, as was right and proper. He was the more experienced; if anyone was to get the *Cossack* out of the trap, it would be the skipper. Now he took over the defence of the *Cossack* against the German infantry and artillery on the shore and the hills above. 'Guns,' he ordered frantically, 'get on to those bloody Jerries!' He snapped at the grizzled old chief petty officer standing by to carry out orders for the deck below, 'Check the damage and report immediately ... Check with the Snotty in charge below. Tell him to issue rifles and to take on the

Jerries in—' He ducked hurriedly as a bullet whined off the steel plating just above his head.

'That nearly parted yer hair, sir,' the CPO said with a grim laugh. He hadn't moved an inch.

Number One forced a laugh. He knew it wouldn't do to let the lower deck see that their officers were rattled. 'You can say that again, Chiefie,' he responded cheerily. 'All right, off you go.'

'Sir.' The CPO swung round as if he were on parade and marched off at a careful stolid pace, as if he had all the time in the world. He too was trying to prove something, this time to the officers and gents.

Half an hour later, the *Kimberley* came steaming out of the fog of war, as the German mortar crews ashore fired bomb after bomb at the trapped destroyer, filling the air with lethal shrapnel which sliced through cables and steel hawsers as if they were made of string. The crews of the two destroyers ignored the danger. Towing hawsers were methodically slung between the two ships. Telegraphs clacked. Ratings shouted orders back and forth through loudhailers.

Now both captain stood on their bridges, disregarding the danger, and personally took charge. Slugs pattered the length of the superstructures as the German infantry spotted that the *Kimberley* was attempting to free the trapped ship by towing her off the rocks. They were out to kill the two captains. In true German fashion, they felt that if they disposed of British officers, their subordinates would go to pieces as usual. Due to the British class system, they reasoned, the lower classes never knew how to take care of themselves in battle.

Both skippers seemed not to notice the danger. As soon as the cables were attached, the captain of the *Cossack* yelled through his loudhailer, 'Prepare to take the strain,' which he followed with a hurried order to the engine room, 'Both astern!' The rescue was under way.

Crouched in the shelter of the chicago piano, holding a tourniquet to his bandaged leg, feeling sick and weak, Wide Boy tried to follow the tricky business. Beneath him on the steel deck plating, the *Cossack*'s engines raced. He could feel the plates trembling violently like a human heart subjected to tremendous strain.

Suddenly there was a colossal jerk. The engine thundered. There was a burst of excited shouts. Wide Boy told himself faintly that this was it. The skipper was giving it max effort.

The Germans on shore seemed to have come to the same conclusion. Now the

159

mortar bombardment was abruptly accompanied by heavy machine-gun fire. Steel ripped the length of the superstructure. Wide Boy ducked the best he could. Suddenly he was afraid, sorry for himself, feeling abandoned, like most wounded men, who feel vunerable once incapacitated. But the feeling passed as swiftly as it had come and he was his old self again, willing the *Cossack* to free itself so that they could be on their way once more and someone might find time to have a look at his wound properly.

But that wasn't to be.

The thunder of the engines pulling astern grew to a crescendo. Now everything was noise: the shriek of the cables, the shouts of the excited, frantic matelots, the chatter of the enemy machine guns interspersed with the hollow boom and obscene thud of the German mortars.

'Come on ... come on, yer bugger ... get on!' Number One cried on the bridge, as the cables between the two ships twanged and sang as they were stretched to their full limits. He pressed his nails into the palms of his hands till they bled. Wouldn't the *Cossack* ever free herself?

Suddenly – startlingly – the foremost cable burst with the crack of a shell exploding. '*Duck!*' someone yelled frantically, as the severed cable cracked back across the battle-littered deck of the trapped destroyer like a great steel whip. One sailor was too late. It sliced his head off in a flash. On it went, tearing and ripping, leaving the sailor's head, complete with steel helmet, to roll into the scuppers like a football abandoned by some careless young schoolkid.

The first rescue attempt had ended in failure. Five minutes later the *Kimberley* was under way again, backing off under a cloud of smoke. The *Cossack* had been abandoned to her fate.

Eight

All that long grey April afternoon they worked their guts out. Under the fire of the *Warspite*'s great 15-inch guns, the German infantry had withdrawn to the reverse slope of the cliffs beyond. But the *Cossack*'s hard-pressed crew knew that once darkness had fallen, the *Warspite* would pull back and the enemy snipers and riflemen would re-appear.

Without too much difficulty, now that they were free to move about the battered, debris-littered deck without danger, the deck hands had erected a derrick. With it they had commenced unloading heavy pieces of unnecessary equipment to lighten the stranded destroyer's load. Anchor and anchor chain went over the side. Shattered boats and the like followed. It was back-breaking work and power from the engines was in short supply, so the captain was forced to use four-man teams, working for at the most fifteen minutes, their faces grey and greasy with strain and sweat as they

162

hauled up the gear by ratchet and lever. Gasping and choking like old men in the throes of a fatal attack of asthma, the teams collapsed when relieved and slumped to the deck as if they would never get up again.

At four that afternoon, work ceased as the captain tried once more to pull the *Cossack* off the rocks. The engines pulled astern, growing in power as the destroyer refused to obey. Madly the screws churned the water into a white fury. The noise was ear-splitting. Lying in his black congealed blood, a weakening Wide Boy held his free hand to one ear, trying to blot out that tremendous sound. He felt he would faint at any moment. But that wasn't to be. Neither could that powerful thrust astern free the trapped craft.

In the end the captain ordered the engines silenced and Number One clambered down below to confer with the frustrated engineer officer, his white overalls filthy with oil stains and dirt. He was red with fury and frustration and in his rage he was almost incomprehensible to Number One as he ranted about the situation. 'I couldnae even greet at it all ... Yon bluidy hole–' he indicated the great jagged rent in the *Cossack*'s bow torn by the rocks on which she was trapped – 'is the frigging trouble, ye ken.'

'I ken.' Number One tried, but irony was

wasted on the puce-faced Scot, who explained that the only way to float the stricken destroyer, in his opinion, was to clean out the water and apply a 'patch'.

Number One was appalled. A 'patch', a rough-and-ready plug made of anything that would do the job, often took hours to build up over a hole if it was going to hold, and he knew they had perhaps only an hour or two left before the grey gloom which passed for night in these northern climes would fall and the *Warspite* and her protective broadsides would be gone. But he put a brave face on it. 'Okey-dokey, Chief,' he winked, though the Scot didn't respond, 'put it in, as the actress said to the bishop. But as quick as possible ... I'll give you all the men I can spare.'

With that he was gone, praying harder than he had ever done since a kid at prep school, bidding God to let him pass the exam into Dartmouth.

By six, the engine room crew were virtually exhausted. It was now that the chief petty officer asked for volunteers from the off-duty watch. The HO men, however, were uncertain. The older hands had told them that any matelot in his right mind never volunteered in the Royal; and there were too few regulars to make a patch work. Then, however, to everyone's open-mouthed amazement, Scouse – of all people – raised his right hand and said, 'I'll go.'

The assembly's mouths dropped open. 'Cor fuck a duck,' someone gasped. 'Fancy old Scouse volunteering! They'll be telling me next that frigging Father Christmas is real!'

But that April evening, with the *Cossack* totally on her own, trapped in enemy waters with the German infantry waiting ready to attack as soon as the *Warspite* had departed, the men of the *Cossack* all felt like that. Regulars and conscripts, heroes and cowards – all of them were prepared to save not just their own hides, but that of the ship, too. For the *Cossack* had become their home, their family, their country – the very reason for their fighting. Now nothing seemed to matter but the saving of HMS *Cossack*.

Even Wide Boy, that one time cynical spiv, felt the same. Half delirious with his wound, wrapped in his own and Number One's duffle coat, he was perched once more behind his chicago piano, fighting desperately not to lapse into unconsciousness, telling himself that someone had to guard the deck, while the others did their best to free the ship. 'Come on,' he babbled, eyes unfocused, seeing double most of the time, 'come on, yer German fuckers. Let me show what's waiting for you. Come on...' His cries vanished into the night as, a mile away, red signal flares rose into the sky above the *Warspite* and her guns ceased thundering: the signal for her departure. The *Cossack* was alone at last.

The German mountain infantry came out of the hills silently, slowly, cautiously, like grey predatory timber wolves, scenting their prey. They slipped from rock to rock noiselessly, trained alpinists as they were. Indeed, all their equipment was muffled and silenced for just this kind of attack, which was more a kind of lethal infiltration than an organised infantry attack with startlines, timed objectives and all the rest of the usual battalion staff planning. They were helped too by the persistent hollow boom of hammering coming from the trapped destroyer below, which sounded, as if it were a sheet metal plant rather than a deadly fighting ship that could annihilate them if they were caught defenceless in the open. But that wasn't going to happen. Metre by metre they crept ever closer.

Down below next to the torn ripped hull, through which the matelots of the *Cossack* could see the shadowy outline of the cliff wall beyond, they were well into the wearisome, even physically brutal task of constructing the patch. It entailed building a wall of planks, fashioned by the ship's chippy, across the gaping hole. These planks would be secured at each end by what the matelots called 'walking sticks', or iron rods. Eventually the walking sticks would be caulked by the 'pudding', a roll of packing-filled canvas.

Naturally the process was as unfamiliar to the HO men as it would be to any land-lubber. All the same, under the guidance of the engine-room petty officers and arti-ficers, they worked all out to get the unusual job done. The water unfortunately came up to their waists and in that arctic clime it was freezing and chilled them to the bone so that at the end of a ten-minute spell at the job they had to be hauled out, pitiful shells of ashen-faced youths who had to be thawed out before they suffered from frostbite of their nether limbs.

But time and time again they returned to face that cruel cold. Scouse was a tower of strength. He took two shifts in succession, snarling, when the CPO ordered him to get out of the water, 'Leave it off, Chiefie. I know what I'm fookin' doing.' To which the latter replied, 'I do too, son. Yer goolies are gonna fall off if yer stay down in the freezing water much longer.' But seemingly Scouse was prepared to risk that terrible fate. He laboured on.

Back in England, other young men returned from their soccer matches, smoked their 'Woods' and looked forward to a night in the local 'palais de danse', and their girls curled their hair with tongs in front of coal fires, hoping they might be taken to the 'flicks' first, while *these* young men worked for their very lives, unknown to an England still preoccupied with a 'phoney war'. Even when they were dead and mostly forgotten, save by their dear ones, no one would really know what these nineteen- and twenty-year-olds had undergone. Why should they? The world of the fighting man was a closed book to the general run of civilians; it always would be thus...

The first shot rang out like a brittle stick being snapped underfoot in a bone-dry summer wood. The bullet slammed into the metal just above Wide Boy's head. There was a sudden flurry of angry blue sparks. A sudden stink of burned metal. Then they were rushing the jetty to the rocks, firing from the hip as they did. Vaguely Wide Boy heard their wild cries. 'Alles fur Deutschland! Alles fur den Führer!' He shook his head like a man trying to wake from a deep sleep. Suddenly everything came into vision. The Germans charging in their ski caps. The scarlet flashes of their machine guns on the heights and the renewed hollow boom of their mortars, with the bombs already shrieking as they plummeted down on the trapped destroyer.

He pressed his trigger, but the chicago piano was set too high to be really effective. Already its tracer was zipping harmlessly over the heads of the attackers. But Wide Boy knew that it might have a deterrent effect. At the same time, it would rally the frightened young HO, lining the deck to his left and right, trying to aim their unaccustomed rifles. In an instant they too opened fire and the darkness was abruptly stabbed scarlet everywhere by the hectic to and fro of firing.

Here and there, outlined momentarily in a flash of fire, a German threw up his hands in wild melodramatic agony. Next moment the trooper would slap to the ground. Everywhere on the land there were groans, cries, orders, counter-orders and that persistent plea for: 'Sanitater ... stretcher-bearer ... Um Gotteswilles – Sanitater hieruber!' But despite the casualties the attackers were beginning to take, they were skilled experienced infantry. They kept on coming, using whatever cover there was skilfully, dodging from rock to rock, exposing themselves for only a fleeting second before going to ground again. Behind his massed machine guns, the empty cartridge cases clattering down in a golden, steaming rain, Wide Boy knew that once the Germans had got under the cover of the smashed bow, that would be it. They would swarm up in the dead ground afforded by the ship and deal with the inexperienced matelots. He flung a mad prayer to heaven. 'God, help us ... *PLEASE!*' The uneven battle continued.

Down below the patch was almost ready. The men in the water paused, almost exhausted, and gazed up at Number One standing there in his dripping long johns (for he too had taken a spell down in the watery pit helping to complete the patch). 'A couple of small cheers?' one of the regulars gasped. 'I think she'll hold, sir.'

'Two!' Number One forced himself to say, putting all the rest of his energy in his words. 'No, three ruddy great ones ... Yes, lads, let's try it.'

'After you, Claud.' A mimic imitated the two naval characters from Tommy Handley's *ITMA*. 'No, after *you*, Cecil...' They all laughed. They knew what he meant. For after that interchange would always come, 'Spare a penny for the diver, sir.' But there'd be no pennies for them. They'd be heading right for the bottom of the fjord if the patch failed once they had cleared the rocks.

Now, however, a weary Number One had no time for such dire thoughts. In the momentary silence in the hold he could hear the angry snap and crackle of the small arms fire up top, and he didn't need a crystal ball to realise that the Huns were attacking in strength. They had to get out while they still had a chance.

Now, ignoring the ever closer firing coming from the rocks, the rest of the crew got on with the tricky business of getting the stranded ship away while there was still time, while down below the engine-room crew kept their eyes on the patch and tended to their engines, as if they were dealing with very sensitive and delicate instruments indeed. Which was true; they were. Even the most junior engine-room artificer knew that the slightest sudden increase in pressure on the hull meant the patch would burst and the *Cossack* would be sinking, out of control. Suddenly, the more imaginative of the engine-room crew started to sweat with the tension of it all.

Sheltering the best he could behind the stanchions of the battle-littered deck, with bullets whining off the superstructure on all sides, Number One was in contact with the skipper on the bridge by loudhailer, while the latter relayed whatever directions he had to give to the engine room below.

'All right, we're going to try, Number One,' the captain called above the angry racket of the fire-fight. 'Engine room – nice and gently now ... Let's say thirty revs.'

Number One tensed as he heard the increased whine of the turbines. He was sweating despite the intense cold. A bead of sweat was trickling unpleasantly down the small of his back. It was now or never, he knew. He heard the clatter of the bridge telegraph and read the signal, 'Slow astern'. They were off.

There was a teeth-grinding rending of metal as the ship started to come clear of the rocks. A slight tremor. Down below something came loose with a metallic clang. Number One prayed it wasn't the patch. It wasn't. The speed increased ever so slightly. He was pouring with sweat now. Down below the efforts of the German alpine infantry intensified. They knew they were going to be cheated of their prey if they didn't watch out. A machine gun started to spit fire at close quarters with a high-pitched hysterical hiss. Slugs flew everywhere. Yet another matelot went down, a pattern of red holes from which blood arced stitched across his skinny chest. He trampled and kicked with his feet like a spoiled child in a tantrum for a few moments, then lay still. Instinctively Number One knew he was dead.

Then it happened. The *Cossack* lurched to port. It caught Number One off guard. He stumbled and almost fell. The angry curse died on his lips. She was afloat, freed from the rocks. 'Hurrah!' he yelled to no one in particular. Now her speed increased, perhaps by a mere couple of knots. But she was definitely moving backwards at a faster rate.

Number One pulled himself together. 'All's well down here, sir,' he cried through the loudhailer at the shadowy figure of the captain on the bridge.

'Good show, Number One,' the captain called back, pulling his fur hat more tightly down on his head.

The Germans had already reached the shattered bow, however. One of them attempted to leap up and grab the jagged metal. He was a brave but foolish man. Number One fired without aiming. The revolver leapt in his left hand. The man screamed desperately. For a moment it seemed he might be able to hang on to his hold. But that wasn't to be. He fell screaming right beneath the *Cossack*'s bows. Number One closed his eyes momentarily; he didn't want to see the bloody pulp to which he knew the alpine trooper's body would be reduced.

Now the German fire intensified furiously. The land troops realised that the Tommies were making their last attempt to escape. That was something that General Dietl, the head of the alpine troops and a fanatical follower of the Führer, wouldn't allow. He needed the kudos of capturing an enemy destroyer. What headlines that would make! 'Mountain Troops Take Tommy Warship'! It was unheard of.

The men were behind their lean, buck-toothed general too. They were half starved, short of rations since they had been cut off in this God forsaken place, and they knew the Tommy ship would be packed high with delicacies. To fight for 'Folk, Fatherland and Führer', as the popular slogan of the day had it, didn't mean much to them. They preferred to battle for corned beef, cognac and good Tommy cigarettes!

So they made a last desperate effort. The light mountain guns were ordered down to tackle the escaping vessel at close range. The troopers had long lost their mules, but they set to work with a will, hauling the 75mm, short-barrelled weapons by brute force. The mortar crews intensified their barrage, half deafened as shell after shell erupted from the red-glowing barrels of their mortars. All was noise, rage and scarlet fury.

The blow when it came caught Wide Boy

completely by surprise. Perhaps he was still dazed from the loss of blood from his leg wound. Otherwise he might have heard the howl of the mortar bomb descending and ducked. But he didn't.

Suddenly his world erupted in a burst of angry light. It blinded him. He gasped, but not with pain. Instead it was surprise and shock that this was happening to him. For he found himself being torn from his steel-and-leather seat at the machine guns and, for some reason which he couldn't quite fathom, being whirled effortlessly through the air to the accompaniment of ammunition exploding all around like some crazy firework display on Bonfire Night. Next moment the pace quickened. He was slammed against the bulkhead, as if propelled there by a punch from a gigantic fist. For what seemed an age he was pinned there, unable to move, his vision disappearing and reappearing in multicoloured confusion. Then he screamed with pain and started to slip to the floor, trailing a streak of his own bright red blood behind him snail-like on the metal of the bulkhead.

Even as consciousness slipped away weakly, a slow smile spread across his ashen face as he heard the increasing throb of the engines and felt the vibrant trembling under his blood-filled shoes. The old *Cossack* had bloody well made it. They were going home. Back to England. Then the black veil of unconsciousness slipped down in front of his eyes and he knew no more.

1940/41

There was jam, jam ... mixed up with the ham
In the quartermaster's store.
My eyes are dim, I cannot see,
I have not brought my specs with me...
        Camp concert ditty, 1940/41

One

He existed in a white haze. Occasionally the whiteness seemed to turn to a fiery scarlet. Then he felt the pain. His arm was taken. A sudden sharp odour assailed his nostrils. Sometimes he blinked tears. Not for long. A prick in his upper arm. An abrupt feeling of nausea. The pain vanished. He returned to the white haze.

Most of the time in the white haze he hovered – he realised afterwards – on the border between consciousness and oblivion. In the former state he could make out hazy white shapes that moved totally noiselessly, as if they did not possess legs. Voices, when he was conscious enough to make them out, came from very far away. They urged him – and they seemed to be female – to 'swallow this ... try this' and ended always with a standard remark, 'Now that's a good boy.' It was the same when they shoved something cold and metallic under his buttocks and waited and when they spoke, he felt his mother was present and encouraging him to

179

'give me a number one'.

When he wasn't aware of the white haze, he realised weeks afterwards, he had been submerged in a drug-sleep, being wakened not by those shadowy, gliding figures in white, but by his own harsh snoring. Then he would turn, mutter 'sorry' and immediately commence snoring again. But when he did sleep, snoring was not his only activity. He dreamed. How he dreamed! Wild and wonderful dreams of the war, his childhood, a boat, even sex. Once when he dreamed of the latter – a girl against a wall, with his penis right up her, her urging him on, both of them panting crazily, he came back to that white haze and a gentle female voice saying, 'It's all right ... all right, Wilson ... you're getting better.' And he was half certain that someone had touched him down there. For he had felt a sense of relief and wetness and someone wiping him so that he could turn over and begin snoring once more.

How long he existed in this strange remote white world, he didn't know. Later, after he had come out of his coma, they told him that it had been nearly a month. It might have been. It didn't matter. He had enjoyed it and, even half conscious, as he was towards the end of this period out of life and the war, he had felt happy – happy and without responsibilities.

Outside in that remote world of which he caught only glimpses – a sudden fire, loud banging noises, an occasional, panicked rush of stretcher-bearers hurrying in casualties, he knew not from what battle, their stretchers dripping blood – the phoney war had at last been transformed into a shooting war. France and the Low Countries had been overrun and defeated in a matter of a few short weeks. The Germans had ejected the British from the Continent, chasing them out lock, stock and barrel at a place called Dunkirk. Once a nurse put a newspaper into his trembling hands and when he muttered that he couldn't read it (though he could just make out the grinning Tommy with his bandaged head giving the thumbs-up salute), she read the front page for him, full of 'Bravo BEF ... Thumbs up, folks ... Thank you, boys' and all the other propaganda slogans.

Then the nurse had to rush off to empty the bedpan of the sailor who was bleeding from two orifices and he retired back to that warm white world again, the *Daily Mirror* resting on his chest. When he came to again, it was gone, as was the sailor, and nobody had time to read a paper to him again. Not that he minded, if he was ever sure that someone *had* read the news to him. He liked his remote, clean, warm, white retreat.

But Wide Boy couldn't altogether escape the war. Some time that summer, as the *Luftwaffe* turned its hand to bombing the coastal areas in preparation for the coming invasion, Portsmouth's Hasler Naval Hospital was evacuated of its long-term casualties to make way for the new ones the authorities expected. Naturally Wide Boy knew little of all this. All he knew was that he was given an injection and carried into an ambulance as the Stukas started to fall out of the sky over Southsea, to wake up sore and bruised from the long journey over poor second-class roads in a room filled with the salty tang of sea air.

For what seemed an age, he was content to settle into the tiny room which had been allotted to him, his only contact with the outer world the visits from the flustered overworked nurses who all spoke with the slow, deliberate accent of the East Yorkshire coast. He didn't mind. It was summer and the window was left open during daylight, and he was quite happy to lie there in an almost permanent daydream, listening to the roar and grind of the shingle on the beach some hundred-odd yards away and the crisp hobnailed stamp of the infantry platoons on their way to man the beach defences. Once he dreamed he heard music

– the kind he had danced to himself in another age. But it was late at night when he thought he had heard the music and afterwards he told himself that it was yet another of those pleasant idle dreams that filled his days and nights these days. Still he wondered. But he didn't ask about the music. There was no one, it seemed, who had time to answer his questions, even if he had posed them, which he wasn't inclined to do. So he forgot the matter and fell into other dreams, enjoying the warm air coming through the open window of the little provincial cottage hospital and the soothing to and fro of the breakers on the pebble shingle.

Some time that summer, however, Wide Boy was brought into contact once more with the war, which he had forgotten and which, he believed, had forgotten him. It was a Sunday morning – of what month he never found out. But he knew it was Sunday from the sound of the organ coming through the open door of the twelfth-century church some hundred yards or so from the cottage hospital, and the unaccustomed chatter of many voices, those of the churchgoers having a good gossip after the service.

It was about then that Nurse Peters, a pretty woman of about twenty-eight, whose husband was with the army in the Middle East, surprised him with, 'Now I'm going to do your bed up again, Wilson, and you'd better stay awake afterwards.' He looked up and she looked down with assumed sternness, which was belied by the twinkle in her bright blue warm eyes. 'Yes, stay awake. You've got visitors at eleven from Hull. Shipmates they say they are ... But to me they look more like pirates.' And before he had time to ask questions, she had whisked him to one side and was redoing his bed with that trained swift expertise of hers.

'Hello, shipmate ... cushy ruddy number ye've got here, matey ... Fuckin' hell, look at them grapes ... excuse me frigging French, sister...' They came bouncing in, all full of that typical sailor's joie de vivre, chattering away, making lewd comments, stubbing out their cigarettes and placing the cigarette ends behind their right ears, thrusting their caps to the back of their greased hair in non-regulation fashion: British Royal Navy matelots at their best, as if they hadn't a care in the world, their lives seemingly one long round of 'beer and bints'.

Wide Boy stared at them, open-mouthed, unable to speak, while 'Sister Peters', as they called her, promoting her a rank, patted his bed – and him – at regular intervals, as if she wished to prove to them just what a fine job she had done on their grievously wounded shipmate.

Then came the gifts. As they explained to him, they had found him here just by chance. They'd come to a dance at the nearby Queen's Hotel (now he realised where the music had come from; it wasn't just a figment of his imagination). 'Cor fuck a duck, as soon as the local Judies saw us, all tiddly in our best blues, the brown jobs' – they meant the local soldiers – 'didn't stand a cat's chance in hell.' Apparently one of the 'local judies' had explained that there was a lonely grievously wounded sailor lying in the nearby hospital. They had enquired, found it was a member of the *Cossack*'s crew, guessed it was him and decided, on this last day before they sailed again from Hull, they'd come and see him 'before the boozers opened'.

Now they dumped their presents on his bed – a tin of fifty Capstans, duty free; two bottles of Bass Light Ale 'nicked from the stores'; Saturday's *Daily Mirror* with Jane stripped to her cami-knickers yet again. 'If you turn her around, you can just see her pubic hair beneath her knicks...' While Nurse Peters looked on a little helplessly, they started to smoke, offering him the forbidden 'gaspers' and a 'wee nip' from the

185

flask which they thought they could hide from her view.

Even Scouse, sporting his three red stripes and the ribbon of his DCM, had come with the rest. He didn't say much, but at least he didn't scowl, and when it came to his turn to have a swift swig of the illicit stolen rum he wiped the flask afterwards before handing it to a helpless Wide Boy, who didn't seem to know what to do with it. At least it showed he was in some way concerned about the condition of the man with whom he had once requested a 'grudge fight' from Number One, in what now seemed another age.

But then they were gone and, as Nurse Peters fanned the air with their copy of the *Daily Mirror* to rid the room of cigarette smoke and rum fumes before the matron made her rounds, Wide Boy heard Scouse, outside in the corridor preparing for their sally to the local boozer, say, 'Well, we'll never see him on the old *Cossack* agen.'

Someone must have objected, for Scouse added, 'Ner, take it from me, mates, he'll never manage that grudge fight ... all that cockney piss and vinegar has gone.' Then they were gone too. Slowly a solitary tear started to run down Wide Boy's pale sunken cheek.

★ ★ ★

One week later HMS *Cossack* set sail for the Mediterranean and the violent new battles that had begun to rage in that warm inland sea. Behind them Wide Boy languished in that remote East Yorkshire hospital, while the Board in faraway London decided whether or not he should be discharged. As Nurse Peters told her patient confidentially, 'You're a problem, you know, Wilson.'

'How a problem?'

'Well, the local medics think you might be swinging the lead, trying to work your ticket—' Before he could attempt a feeble protest, she added, 'I can understand them. Your wounds are well healed. So why is it you are still not feeling well enough to get on your feet and start to regain your strength.' She looked down at them. 'You know,' she said slowly, 'it might be all up here.' She tapped her right temple.

'But I'm not mental, Nurse,' he stuttered, suddenly aghast. For him, as for so many of his time and class, mental illness was the greatest of stigmas. 'I'm just—'

She put out her hand instinctively and smothered his words. 'Of course you're not,' she reassured him and he caught the scent of her hand. It smelled of cool cleanliness, expensive soap. It was very reassuring. Then she bent down and kissed him. On the lips!

187

Before he could say another word, she had vanished, leaving his mind in the kind of whirl that he had not experienced since those last desperate minutes on the rocks in the fjord at Narvik.

Two

The *Cossack* sailed for the Med, as the matelots always called it, and arrived at 'Gib', or 'the Rock', as they named the naval base guarding the entrance to the inland sea, just in time to take on the Italians, who were unleashing the full force of their naval power in that area. In the late summer of 1940 Mussolini had over two hundred thousand men in North Africa ready to march into Egypt and capture Cairo. In the East African colonies he had an even greater army, which had already invaded British Somaliland and was throwing back the inferior British forces, which consisted of native levies officered by a handful of whites. Everything seemed to be going the Italian dictator's way and, when the defeated French fleet failed to leave their African and Mediterranean ports and continue the war against the Axis under the new Free French leader, de Gaulle, it appeared that Mussolini's vaunted 'Italian lake', the *Mare*

Nostrum, was well and truly under Italian control.

But the bombastic, boastful Italian Duce had not reckoned with a handful of British captains, who were as resourceful and as aggressive as Nelson's sea dogs had been when they had faced up to – and beaten – a much more powerful and cunning dictator, Napoleon, more than a hundred years before in these selfsame waters. The skippers of those ancient Great War battleships, the *Warspite*, the *Valiant*, the *Queen Elizabeth* and the rest, barely protected by the handful of Fleet Air Alarm planes, most of them antiquated two-wingers, were quite prepared to take on fast Italian cruisers and battleships half their age. Once again it was the same old story of British courage, cunning and craft having to make up for two decades of starving the Royal Navy of funds and new ships.

But the great sea captains knew they had to have supplies to be able to continue fighting; and the merchantmen which brought in these supplies to the key British naval bases of Malta and Alexandria had to be protected. And it was here that swift, lean destroyers such as *Cossack* and the rest of the Tribal class came into their own.

Unlike the capital ships with their crews of thousands, which had to keep up speed to survive and could not be sacrificed for the sake of a convoy-load of petrol or even dehydrated potatoes and dried eggs, the destroyers could be sunk – and were – without greatly affecting the morale of the folk back home. The destroyers, with their crews of a couple of hundred or so, could risk being bombed or torpedoed at slow speed, fighting off attacking subs or surface craft without air cover or heavy ship support. Thus it was that the crews of ships like HMS *Cossack* knew when they received their orders to sail to the Med to protect a convoy of merchantmen for Malta or Alexandria that they were taking their lives into their hands; that they were being sent on what amounted to a suicide mission. Once the Italians and, increasingly, the Germans too, picked up their presence at Gib, the destroyer sailors knew that their lives would rest in the lap of the gods. Anything could happen, from sub and surface attacks to Italian daredevils riding high-explosive human torpedoes and attempting to sink them even before they left port. In the Med, their lives were numbered not in weeks, but, in many cases, simply in days.

The *Cossack* came under submarine attack almost immediately. By now the destroyer which had breached Norwegian territorial waters to release the *Altmark*'s prisoners was well known to Admiral Raeder and the German Naval High Command. The sheer affrontery of the act and the way that the Tommy destroyer had escaped the Narvik trap had angered him considerably. When he learned that the *Cossack* had passed through the Straits of Gibraltar, he requested the Italian naval authorities at Bari to ensure that they took immediate action against the enemy ship. As he snapped to the German naval liaison officer in his no-nonsense manner over the scrambler phone in Berlin, 'Kapitanleutnant, tell those tame Macaronis of yours that the Führer desires that piece-of-shit destroyer, the *Cossack*, destroyed at the first available opportunity. Is that clear?'

'Jawohl, Herr Grossadmiral,' the cocky young lieutenant-commander had replied and then, wondering yet again how irate these old admirals got, he changed into his number one uniform to go over to the 'Macaronis' to present his compliments and convey the supposed 'Führer's request'.

Professional and full of confidence that they had the Duce's *Mare Nostrum* fully under control as the Italian officers were, they waited till their spies in Spain and in the sunken tanker with its secret chamber just off Gibraltar reported that the *Cossack* was about to sail with a convoy bound for Malta. Then they snapped into action.

Two submarines – the Duce himself had ordered there should be no slip-up; in the honour of his 'revolutionary comrade', Adolf Hitler, there would be two underwater attackers – were dispatched to rendezvous south of Sicily and then sail towards the North African coast to the general area of British convoys, keeping as far away as possible from the Italian airfields in the south of that country.

There they positioned themselves, two of the most modern subs in the world, and waited till the convoy hove into sight. At an average speed of approximately eight knots an hour, they would have time to carry out the plan of attack already worked out at HQ in Bari. As the senior Italian submarine commander, Commandante Rizzi, radioed his colleague just after they had taken up their positions, 'There'll be at least the German Iron Cross Second Class in it for you, Angelo.'

'Si, Signor Commandante,' his colleague had answered dutifully, telling himself that he knew now who would be getting the German Iron Cross, First Class. But for once the eager young submarine skipper with his dashing pointed beard and flashing black eyes, both of which made him look like a pirate, was wrong.

They sighted the convoy on the surface in bright moonlight. It was perfectly still off the coast of North Africa and they could hear the steady throb of the English ships quite clearly, although they were several kilometres away. Carefully Commandante Rizzi surveyed the slow procession of tankers and merchantmen plodding steadily forward in a north-easterly direction bound for Malta. From below the operators reported a steady pinging noise. Someone was echo-ranging, and merchantmen didn't have echo-ranging equipment. The sounds were coming from the convoy's escorts.

Promptly the commandante ordered the submarine to submerge, knowing that Angelo would already be moving into the convoy to knock out a tanker and start the escorts off on the hunt for the supposed lone attacker. Then he would bring his own boat into play to look for the *Cossack*. If the English destroyer remained with the convoy, which he thought she would as a guard, she'd be easy meat at convoy speed. He beamed as he prepared to slide down the ladder into the fetid, evil-smelling interior of the sub. Naturally, once he had sunk the *Cossack*, he'd be a national hero. The Duce would see to that. After his recent defeat in the desert, Mussolini needed all the good publicity he could get. The commandante smirked and stroked his beard, telling himself he'd have to have it dyed jet black once again as soon as he got back to base. He couldn't appear in Rome for the award ceremony with his grey hairs showing through. After all, he was one of Mussolini's 'sons of the wolf'.

Although they had been expecting it, the officers of the *Cossack*, enjoying their off-watch time in the wardroom, sipping at their pink gins, were caught by surprise by the explosion. One moment everything was steady, routine, peaceful; the next all hell was let loose as the tanker a mile away went up in a great oily blue whoosh of flame, which turned into a gigantic searing blow-torch that swept the length of the tanker's long deck, greedily burning up everything in front of it. Suddenly, all was noise – bells jingling, sirens shrieking, rattles turning – confusion, and white-hot anger.

Madly scrambling into their helmets and duffle coats (for it was cold at night still in the Mediterranean), the officers flung themselves outside, their faces suddenly hollowed out into scarlet death's heads by the flames of the fiercely burning tanker. For a moment they gasped in shocked awe. Tiny burning human torches were flinging themselves over the sides of the tanker while

195

they could, while other burning figures were trying desperately to lower boats. But in vain. They were turned into charred pygmies before they could do so.

The spell was broken. Madly the officers ran to their duty stations as the other escorts broke station and the freighters attempted to do the same while the convoy commodore signalled with his aldis lamp that they had to keep position. Moments later the skipper of the *Cossack* was ordered to keep station with the convoy and be on the lookout for a further sub attack, while the other escorts ran a sweep.

When Scouse heard the order in A turret, he picked his nose calmly and growled, 'Then we've nowt to worry about, have we? Them Eyeties would rather fuck than fight.' It was a pious hope.

Now, with the other destroyers and corvettes departed, the *Cossack*'s crew felt that strange eerie sensation they'd experienced before when dealing with subs: the uncanny feeling that beneath them, perhaps directly under their own hull, there lurked the unseen killer. It was a mood that was increased by the high silver moon which now bathed the low drifting fog in its spectral light. Now everything seemed heavy, ponderous and threatening. Orders were given in low voices and even when the crew spoke to one another they kept their words in a subdued tone, almost as if the enemy sub skipper was just behind them, listening to what they were saying.

And, of course, in a way, Commandante Rizzi was. He had already ordered 'silent running', and in the unnatural red light of the submerged craft the crew whispered to one another when it was necessary to say something, while the operators strained at their earphones, trying to catch the slightest sound from above. Rizzi knew that his skilled operators could easily pick up the noise of a destroyer's engines from that of a slow, ponderous, antiquated freighter. He ordered in a low, tense voice, 'Up periscope!'

The steel tube sped upwards almost noiselessly. The commandante turned his ornate gold-braided cap back to front so that he could get closer to the scope. Next to him, the lieutenant stood ready with the warship identification book, a series of silhouettes of British warships from battlecruiser to destroyer.

Carefully Rizzi turned the tube round. He stopped. Next to him the young officer with the book tensed. Rizzi turned up the enhancer.

'Sir?'

Rizzi didn't reply immediately. He peered

hard and then flung a quick glance at the silhouette presented to him by the officer at his side. 'Si ... il *Cossack*,' he rasped, voice filled with excitement. 'We attack!'

Up ahead in the *Cossack*, the crew waited for the inevitable. They knew someone was 'gonna get a packet', as Scouse expressed it. 'It stands to reason, mates.' It did. If the Italians had started hunting in 'wolf packs', as the Germans did, they would have more than one sub concentrating on the Malta convoy. Now the other escorts had been drawn away, it would be as easy as falling off a log for the Italians to launch a 'tin fish' at one of the now relatively unprotected merchantmen. 'Right up the Khyber Pass,' as Scouse reminded his tense listeners.

Now every man available watched and waited in tense expectation. On the bridge they scoured the surrounding water for the first sign of a second enemy. On the deck they did the same, with the depth-charge crews ready for action at a moment's notice, while below decks the operators hunched over their sets, listening to the ping-ping of echo-sounding or peering at the green-glowing radar screens, watching for the first hazy white dots that could mean an instant call to action.

Then it happened. A sudden mind-rending shudder. It began amidships and worked its way aft. Now it was growing apace. It rattled through every compartment, accompanied by a gushing wind which flung men to the deck, tossing them from bulkhead to bulkhead like caroming billiard balls. Gear showered down in sudden avalanches. The hammocks swung wildly.

Below in the engine room, dials splintered. Lights bulbs popped like firecrackers. Steel fixtures bent and snapped as if they were made of plastic. There was a dull moan followed an instant later by a sudden rush of scalding steam from a ruptured pipe. A stoker screamed high and hysterical. The flesh was flayed from his naked upper body. Abruptly it was transformed into a suppurating pink mess. A petty officer came rushing to help the screaming man. In the half-gloom he ran straight into the high-powered jet of escaping steam. His face slipped down his jaw to his chest like red molten wax. He didn't even have time to scream.

On the bridge, Number One yelled, as the *Cossack* took on a list to port, 'All hands to—' The rest of his words were drowned by A turret opening fire. Even in this moment of supposed disaster, Number One gave a little cry of triumph. The gunners had spotted their assailant – a submarine low in the water, but already swinging round to fire its aft torpedoes. Scouse was at it again.

Down below in the Italian submarine, the crew had stopped their wild cheering at the success of their first 'fan' of bow torpedoes. Two had missed and three had failed, probably for some technical reason, but the last had definitely hit the *Cossack*. Even with the naked eye the bridge group could see, outlined a stark black in the flames which were beginning to creep up along the destroyer's deck, that she was listing. Now all that Rizzi had to do was to slam his aft torpedoes into her or just close enough to buckle her hull plates and that Iron Cross, First Class and the trip to Rome would be his.

His handsome face gleamed with triumph as he rapped out his orders to the torpedo officer. He wanted the young officer candidate to carry out the task slowly and efficiently. They had plenty of time. The other escorts were well away by now following Angelo and undoubtedly the British would be panicking aboard the *Cossack*. He had all the time in the world.

'Wait for my instruction,' he said patiently. 'I don't want you to fire without—'

The sharp crack and boom alerted him to the sudden danger. He jerked his head up above the protective rim of the conning tower. A furious white blur was zipping madly across the sea towards the submarine. He shrieked in panic in that same instant that the whole world in front of him erupted in an all-consuming deafening white flame. The curse died in his throat as his head was wrenched from his neck in one great tearing, agonising heave and went skidding over the side, undyed beard and all.

Three

She had come to his hospital room on the Saturday night, after the visit of Scouse and the rest from the *Cossack*, when he had broken down. Over the road at the Queen's, the dance band of the King's Own Yorkshire Light Infantry was playing some rather staid dance music. To Wide Boy, it seemed, they were playing Sousa marches at a very slow speed indeed. Still, he didn't mind; he couldn't sleep anyway. His mind was still too full of his problems and what he should do next. Had his nerve gone completely? Or could he face active service, with all its dangers, in a fighting ship – the *Cossack*, naturally – once again?

About ten, one hour before the Queen's 'Services Dance – All Our Brave Boys Welcome – Admission Threepence' closed down, there was a soft, careful knock on the door. It surprised him. He never had visitors – who knew he was there – and, of course, the medics never knocked. 'Come in,' he called, somewhat surprised.

He was surprised even more when he recognised his visitor. It was Nurse Peters. She was wearing the regulation Red Cross blue cape and bonnet, but the bonnet was slightly askew and underneath the cape she wore a floral dress. She looked unusually flushed, too, as if she might have been drinking. Later he found out he'd been right. She had.

She winked and said, 'Can I come in for a minute or two? I've got something for you. I know it's naughty. But I think you deserve it. You've really started to pull yourself together this week.' She pulled out a bottle of beer from underneath her cape. 'Best Yorkshire Taddy Ale. Bought it for you at the dance. Thought you ought to have a Saturday night treat, too, all alone up here.' She pouted her lips playfully in a kind of a kiss and suddenly he realised that for an 'old woman', Nurse Peters was quite attractive. 'OK?'

He nodded. He was still not used to speaking much. Indeed, he still found it difficult to string together anything longer than a short phrase.

Hastily she had slipped outside, taken her beer and poured it into the tooth glass, then handed it to him. She sat down carelessly at the side of his bed, and he noticed as she did so that she had nice shapely white thighs above the tops of her obviously best black silk stockings.

She'd watched him, almost like a loving possessive mother watching her child drinking milk, as he sipped the beer greedily. He felt it go to his head immediately.

For a while they had chatted. For the first time in ages, he had enjoyed talking, helped by the influence of the weak Taddy Ale and her presence. Then, despite the fact that she must have washed his naked body scores of times, he had begun to feel the first stirrings of lust – again, it must have been the beer – and he had started to be fascinated by the movement of her silk-clad legs. Every time she shifted them, he followed their every movement.

About eleven the band began its winddown. There was the 'Good Night, Ladies' followed by the Last Waltz, to the accompaniment of beery laughter and singing, which hushed immediately when the KOYLI band became a military one again and solemnly played 'God Save the King'. 'Well, I for one am not standing to attention,' Nurse Peters had joked as the lights had gone out, while outside they had heard the stamp of military hobnail boots, the grind of three-ton trucks starting up to take the soldiers back to their billets and the pitter-patter of high heels as the local girls linked up in fives and sixes (it was safer that way) and set off homewards, trilling into the blackout, 'Now this is number one and he's got her on the run ... roll me over in the clover ... roll me over and do it agen...'

Then there was a sudden awkward silence as she sat and he lay there in the sudden darkness and both wondered what they should do now. Slowly the cottage hospital settled down for the night. The ancient boards creaked and settled once more as they contracted after the heat of the day. On the floor below, the dying soldier who had lost his legs while laying a mine moaned in his sleep – it was more of a whimper. Once or twice they heard the lavatory being flushed on the first floor as one or other of the few nurses on duty went there. They could well have been all alone in the world, the only two human beings alive.

Once she got up to pull back the blackout. The room was flooded with the warm yellow light of the full moon. Out to sea, he could catch a glimpse of pink silent flickering flame. 'Somebody's catching a packet,' he muttered.

She didn't reply. Suddenly she seemed to be sunk in deep thought.

The old church clock chimed the half-hour. The chime seemed to wake her from her reverie. Drily she asked, 'Shall we?' Her voice no longer sounded tipsy, but grave and serious.

'Yes,' he answered.

Then it had happened.

He tried to rise, but she pushed him back gently, kissed him on the cheek and whispered, 'Oh, leave it to me ... I'll look after you.' She bent and he heard the snap of elastic. She dropped her knickers on the floor.

'What—' he began.

Again she hushed him with that, 'Leave it to me.' She had hitched up her skirt and he had caught a glimpse of her pubic hair, which thrilled him like it always had in the old days. She took him in her hand. He hardened. She pressed a little kiss lightly on its tip. 'Now, you *are* being a good boy,' she said, climbing on the bed and, spreading her legs, lowered herself carefully on top of him.

He gasped. But not under her weight. It was the sheer pleasure of the sensation, which he had thought he'd forgotten: that warm, wet, wonderful sensation that made his heart beat rapidly straight away.

'Easy,' she panted, throwing her head back, her hair suddenly loose and trailing down her back. He reached forward to find and fondle her breasts, which strained and seemed to burst out of her blouse. 'Oh, my

God, I need ... this ... God, how I do!' The words came pouring from her gaping mouth as she thrust herself up and down upon him, his weakness forgotten as she concentrated on her own pleasure.

The old metal hospital bed squeaked rustily. Her breathing grew ever more hectic. She tossed her head wildly from side to side as if in some sort of convulsion, strange unintelligible words and gasps escaping from her slack wet mouth, carried away by a crazy unreasoning lust.

Lying below, hardly able to move, but enjoying himself, feeling a sudden pride at the thought of the strength and power of his manhood giving her so much pleasure, Wide Boy realised he was being used. She was in command, riding that rock-hard pillar of his flesh like a mistress commanding a beast. Not that he cared, for he too was beginning to forget reality – the place, the situation, the difference in their ages, the fact that she was married to a man at the front, even the war. All that mattered now was pleasure – his pleasure!

Crazily their passion mounted and mounted. Her breasts, felt under her blouse, firm and fat, were soaked with sweat. When their bellies slapped together in this mad ride to sexual oblivion they were wet, too. The sounds they made were pure animal, guttural and greedy. Their whole world now consisted of the bed beneath them and their two madly writhing bodies.

Suddenly she sobbed. Her body frozen. Her spine arched like a taut bow. He pressed harder. With all his remaining strength, he gave one final mighty thrust. Next moment she opened her mouth to scream. Just in time he freed a hand from her breasts and stifled it. An instant later she collapsed on top of him, crying and gasping and laughing, covering his sweat-lathered crimson face with tiny feather-light kisses in the same instant that he exploded inside her.

Thus it had started. That last week of the dangerous summer of 1940, the two of them lived in a world of their own, the correct, regulated life of nurse and patient during the daylight hours, counting the time until that crazy world of the night could commence.

Outside the Germans marched southwards. They bombed Britain from coast to coast. Refugees from the big cities flooded the little seaside resort. The dances ceased. There were no soldiers to attend them. They were too busy guarding the mined beaches and supervising the erection of pillboxes everywhere on the cliffs. The German invaders were expected daily.

Daily, too, the new prime minister Winston Churchill exhorted the defeated British to keep fighting. Soon that other 'democracy over the seas' would join in and help to win the battle against Hitler. At news time, crowds gathered anxiously to listen to reports of the latest events. The crowds grew even larger when Churchill spoke and assured them that they would 'never surrender'. The numbers of German aircraft downed over Britain were proclaimed like pre-war football scores.

But all this happened without their appearing to know. They were wrapped up too much in each other. Even when the telegram finally arrived at the hospital, having followed Wide Boy over half of the kingdom, announcing that he was the father of a baby boy, that the mother had applied for an allowance and that she was going to name the baby 'Ginger' after Wide Boy's supposed name, it left no impression on him. He was too engrossed in 'Nurse Peters', a name he still used when addressing her. Somehow it seemed *improper* to use her first name, Angela. If Wide Boy had known the meaning of the word, he would have used it for his situation that late summer and autumn. But he didn't. But he was – he was besotted!

For a few hours each day they were able to

escape from the formalities of the hospital, when she 'volunteered' to take him for walks along the deserted beach beyond the minefields and trenches for 'the patient's health'. And walk they did, often for miles, so that his skinny pale legs grew strong and brown again, until they found a spot in the shelter of the cliffs where they could make love unobserved and undisturbed.

Once or twice, when he had taken his 'medicine' – the same old Taddy Ale which she had brought him that first night when she had felt sorry for him (and, she had to admit, sexually excited) – they had bathed in the cold northern sea naked. Still the desire had been so strong that they had made love in the water, watched only by the bemused baby seals, which fled when they splashed too much in their excitement and she had let full rein to those cries of passion and raw lust that she gave when she was allowed to.

But the war wouldn't leave them in peace. It was like a live thing, begrudging them their pleasure, encroaching on their lives slowly but surely. At first it was still remote: the thunder of the anti-aircraft guns over Hull to the south; the German reconnaissance planes circling and circling over the Humber estuary like sinister black hawks waiting for their prey to emerge; the merchant ship burning fiercely on the far horizon, the victim of some prowling U-boat; the weary refugees from the great battered port plodding barefoot through the wet sand with their filthy snivelling kids, laden with the pathetic bits and pieces of what was left of their slum households – and then the dead body...

He recognised it as a matelot immediately. There was no mistaking the red stripes and the flags of a signaller. He lay half buried in the windswept sand, as if he might be asleep – some matelot who had had a skinful at a local pub and, like sailors did, had gone down to the beach to sleep it off before he dare report to barracks. But this was no sleeping drunk. When they had tried to wake him and tell him the tide was coming in and then, when he failed to waken, had turned him over gently, they had seen he was dead. Half his young face had been blown away and what was left had been eaten by the crabs. Softly Wide Boy had taken his bare foot away and let the dead matelot fall back, his ruined face hidden once more.

Naturally they reported their find, but after the police and a couple of military policemen who had a van had removed the corpse – 'probably some poor bugger from that destroyer torpedoed off Spurn Point last week,' one of the elderly police reservists in his steel helmet had opined – the two of them remained behind, staring at the body's impression in the sand, slowly filling up now as the tide began to encroach on the spot. They didn't speak. Perhaps they didn't quite know how to vocalise their thoughts. Both of them knew, however, that the discovery marked an end to their relationship.

That night, she made love to him once again in the little hospital room. She'd bought a half-bottle of scotch on the black market and between them they finished it, not saying much, not even looking at each other. In bed it was different. They went at each other like wild animals. They bit, tore, kissed savagely. His hand gripped her breasts and buttocks brutally, forcing her legs open, mounting her with a snarl, thrusting himself into her wide-open, gaping loins as if he wished to hurt her.

Afterwards, lathered in sweat and sobbing with their exertions, they lay in each other's arms, still drunk but satiated, with all passion spent, saying little save to ask for a light for a cigarette. Together they stared at the ceiling, two small glowing red lights of their cigarettes illuminating the darkness of the room, with the hospital beneath them remote and silent.

Once he opened his mouth as he leaned

above her on his elbow staring at those magnificent naked breasts of hers with their taut brown nipples and began, 'We must—'

But she smothered the rest of his words with her hand and whispered, 'No, let's not talk ... Talk does no good – *now.*'

Thus they fell asleep, to be wakened by the crowing of cocks, for everywhere in the towns now people were keeping chickens again in order to obtain precious unrationed eggs. He shook his head and started as he opened his eyes. She was already staring down at him, her face a strange mix of love, concern and sorrow. He knew why, but he didn't say so. Instead he accepted the cigarette she offered him wordlessly, still not taking her gaze off his young face.

At six thirty, they heard the first clatter of the cleaners' buckets and the clip-clop of the milkman's trap outside as his tired old nag came up the drive to deliver milk to the cottage hospital. She nodded. It was time to get up and for her to go.

He nodded back.

She stepped out of bed, totally naked still, and he cast his eyes on the woman's firm but fleshy body that had given him so much pleasure and new hope in these last few weeks. 'I'll say goodbye,' she declared.

He leaned forward to kiss her. She shook her head, lips tightly compressed. He could see the glint of tears in her eyes and, older and more sensitive after what he had been through, knew she was on the verge of tears. He was abruptly embarrassed. He put out his hand, too. She took it and pressed it hard. 'Goodbye,' she said simply, her voice shaky.

'When ... I'll write.'

She shook her head. 'No,' she answered firmly. 'It's over ... Don't write.'

'But—'

'No buts.'

He nodded and fell silent.

That morning he packed his gear. He was to report to Hull. If the local board passed him fit for active service, he was to be shipped to Portsmouth for overseas posting and, he guessed, with the casualties mounting drastically in the Med, he stood a good chance of returning to the old *Cossack*. An old oppo from the destroyer had told him over the phone that she was currently in dry dock being patched up yet again, so he reckoned he stood a good chance of returning to her once he got on the draft from Pompey.

At ten that morning he set off for the little rural station next to the cottage hospital from whence he would take the train to Hull. More than once he had tried to spot her at work, without luck. Although he was

214

excited suddenly at the prospect of getting into the war once more, still he didn't think it right to leave her just like that. But in the end, he gave up. He shook the matron's hand, something he wouldn't have dared to do a month before, got a kiss from a couple of the nurses, one of whom actually had tears in her eyes, and then he slung his kitbag and gas mask and set off across the path to the little station.

Just before ten as the Hull train, which would take the handful of soldiers and civilians back to the great port, arrived, he took a final look at the cottage hospital. High up under the roof, at the window of the little room which had been his in a world that was already beginning to recede into the past, he saw her: a white face pressed against the window. She might have been a ghost. Then the old locomotive, tugging its third-class carriages wearily as if it were a live thing and would be glad to have a brief rest, came in. The face vanished. Wide Boy would never see Nurse Peters again.

Four

The sun slashed his eyes like a cut from a sharp knife. Hastily Wide Boy dropped his kitbag on the quayside and looking up, shielded his eyes from the blinding glare. Already the sirens were beginning to sound all round Malta's Grand Harbour, being drowned almost immediately by the thunder of the German bombers.

Up high in that brilliant perfect blue sky, he could make out the slow-moving mass formations of the German Heinkel bombers. But it was the swarms of Messerschmitts and squadrons of Stukas which were making the racket. They were coming in at two levels, the Stukas below the bombers, jostling for position before they fell out of the sky in one of their death-defying dives, the fighters zooming in across the sea at mast-top level, their nose cannon already spurting lethal 20mm tracer shells. It was the old tactic to confuse the British gunners. Three different sets of planes at varying speeds and varying heights. If the gunners didn't keep their wits about them, one of the levels would find their target.

And there were plenty of them. The whole of the harbour was packed with merchant shipping, naval vessels and wrecks, for Malta depended virtually totally on sea supply for its survival, now that the Italian and German Air Forces had turned their full fury on the island. Wide Boy, eyes wrinkled against the glare, flashed a look at the *Cossack* in the basin opposite. She looked nothing like the destroyer he remembered. She was battered, painted with zig-zag camouflage paint and her battle scars were all too obvious; and by the looks of the strength in which the enemy was attacking, she might well have more scars before the day was out.

Now as the land and ship-based artillery took up the challenge, the Stukas let the Messerschmitts flash by heading for the ruined city beyond. For what seemed an age, they hovered over the harbour like sinister metal hawks. Then, with frightening suddenness, they flung themselves, one after another, out of the smoke-pocked blue sky. Sirens shrieking, engines howling, they came hurtling down. Shells exploded in furious puffs of smoke all about them. The sky was suddenly filled with a brown network of the exploding shells. They hurtled through it unharmed. Just when it seemed they would run smack into the water, their pilots hit the airbrakes. They staggered visibly, as if they had abruptly run into a brick wall. Almost instantly a profusion of evil little black bombs tumbled from their ugly bellies. Then the Stukas went screaming upwards again, pursued by the evil white morse of tracer shells and bullets, while all around the water of the harbour was tortured into huge whirling white spouts of seawater.

The first wave missed most of their targets save a fat freighter, its decks laden with crates. It reeled under the impact of the bombs like a toy ship poked by a kid with a stick on a pond. Next instant it began to list and sink, the crates sliding one after another, thousands of pounds' worth of key goods, into the sea. Under other circumstances, Wide Boy would have laughed. It was almost comic, especially the way the seamen waved their arms and gesticulated as they tried – in vain – to stop this unusual way of discharging the ship's cargo. But not now. The bombing attack was getting too close to the poor old battered *Cossack*.

Even as he despaired, the young draftee could see the new skipper urging the gunners to ever greater efforts as the full weight of the German attack concentrated on the Grand Harbour.

Now the morning was hideous with the snarl of tortured engines, the shriek of sirens, the thunder of flak and exploding bombs, the crazy chatter of massed machine guns firing all out. A stricken Stuka, trailing black smoke, the pilot behind the shattered canopy blinded by the broken glass, slammed straight into the sea. Another zoomed in at mast height, obviously out of control, the dead pilot slumped over his joystick, crashing into the side of a merchantman and exploding there in a ball of scarlet fire. Next instant the ship's supplementary oil tank went up and she vanished behind a screen of blinding furious flame. A pilot, baling out, dropping through the spider's web of exploding shells and drifting smoke, his plane circling round and round behind him, smacked into a Messerschmitt going full out to disintegrate with the impact like a pulpy overripe scarlet fig.

Squatting there behind a heap of piled Bofors shells, a shocked Wide Boy told himself the scene looked like one out of the end of the world. The whole place had gone crazy, stark raving mad. How had the matelots, brown jobs and the Maltese civvies stuck it out so long, day after day, ever since the Eyeties had entered the war, raid after raid?

219

Now the sirens were sounding the all clear. The enemy planes were heading back to their bases in Sicily to refuel and rearm and come back to bomb again later in the day. On the quayside the ambulances and fire-tenders were racing down the narrow ancient streets towards the harbour, bells jingling, as across from Wide Boy a Norwegian freighter broke in half and sunk slowly, huge obscene bubbles of trapped air exploding on the surface as she went under. Another day in Malta had commenced...

There were plenty of new faces on the *Cossack*, Wide Boy noted as he reported. They were tanned, all of them, but there was a difference to the new boys: their faces were still plump, youthful and confident. Those of the old ones were different. They were hollowed out, shaved to the bone, and their eyes had a certain sheen, as if they might break down and start crying at any moment.

Here and there old hands recognised him and shouted across as he reported. Even Scouse was friendly – for him. He offered Wide Boy his hand, which the latter took somewhat surprised. 'Nice to see you back. Thought you was a goner,' he said. He, too, looked haggard and worn, much older than his handful of years. There was a livid new scar running down the left side of his face.

Wide Boy told himself he looked the real Scouse hood now. But the Liverpudlian's old fire had disappeared. He snarled still, but the teeth had vanished. After the comment about Wide Boy's apparently short future, he said tamely, 'Anyhow, glad to see you back, you cockney bugger. Anybody's welcome from the old *Cossack* after this shower o' shit.' He indicated the new men going about their task of clearing away the rubble and debris of the recent raid.

It was a sentiment that Wide Boy encountered everywhere that morning from the old hands. Even the officers who had survived this far were no different, including an older and less dashing Number One, who looked sick and bore the ribbon of the DSC on his thin chest. He welcomed Wide Boy in place of the new captain, who had gone off into the town to find a fur hat like Vian's in the hope that it would bring him luck. 'I wouldn't like to be in their place,' Number One commented, 'if he comes across any shot-down air crew – he'll eat the Huns for breakfast. The Old Man's got a rare old head of steam up this morning.' He smiled in the pleasant way he had always done, but the warmth was gone; it was a mere memory of another and better time, carried out mechanically without any real feeling.

Just before the short interview was terminated, animation came back into Number One's voice as he leaned forward and cast a quick glance at the porthole, as if he was afraid they might be overheard, before saying, 'I hope you're really fit again, Wilson. Because the *Cossack*'s going to need every experienced hand she can find soon.'

Wide Boy registered the use of the *Cossack*'s name, as if the destroyer was a person and had desires and wishes of her own. But then, perhaps the ship had become more than a steel shell, armed with guns. He said, 'Why exactly, sir?'

'Can't tell you, Wilson. Don't know exactly myself. But I know it's going to be big.' He lowered his voice even further. 'Why, even Old ABC has been over to Valetta to talk about it to the big shots. So you can see this is going to be real top notch stuff.'

As the chief petty officer wheeled him away from Number One's office so that he could change into dungarees to help on deck, Wide Boy felt impressed. It wasn't every day that the Commander-in-Chief Mediterranean, Admiral A. B. Cunningham, briefed lowly destroyer captains.

Buzzes went back and forth as the *Cossack* was prepared for sea again. Buzzes were a feature of sea-going life in the tight and somewhat isolated confines of a destroyer that normally spent more time at sea than in port. 'We're going back to Blighty,' the men said. 'Churchill sez we've done enough. We deserve a spell at home, drinking real ale and getting our legs over...' 'Ner,' they sneered, 'not on yer frigging life! We'll stay out here in the Med till hell freezes over. We're off to North Africa. When the balloon goes up, they're gonna give us rifles and we're gonna tackle 'em as frigging infantry...' '*Blighty! North Africa!* You must be bleeding barmy,' they snorted. 'Ain't yer got a brain in yer noddle? What d'yer use yer frigging head for – to keep yer hat on! ... Stands to reason, mates, we're off to where the slant-eyed maidens live.' That always raised a chuckle and ribald comments about other parts of the ladies in question being slanted too. 'The Far East, mates, that's where we're off to.'

But such buzzes were inevitably wrong, or at the most contained only a grain of truth. Still they kept on coming while, unknown to the sacrifical lambs of the *Cossack*, their future and that of their ship was being discussed at the highest level. Churchill himself had suggested the scenario and although, as usual, his senior naval and army staff officers didn't like it, they knew they had no other alternative but to carry it out. In 1941, as Churchill snorted angrily often enough, 'Every day, gentlemen, we seem to lose another bit of the Empire, and I didn't become the King's First Minister last year to preside over the demise of his empire.' Something had to be done, and naturally it was, even when it sounded to the Chief of the Imperial General Staff, Field Marshal Alan Brooke, like 'a bunch of strategic balls'.

Thus, unknown to the young men of the *Cossack*, strings were being tightened all over the British Empire. Information from spies, traitors to the German cause, the great decoding operation at Bletchley Park – even burnt-black Englishmen disguised in Arab robes deep in the endless waste of North Africa's Western Desert – was being drawn in to form the 'big picture' which staff officers dearly loved.

But it wasn't a 'big picture' which particularly pleased the new prime minister in London. Russia was now in the war, taking some of the pressure off Britain which had stood alone since June 1940. But the Russians were doing very badly, and anyway Churchill didn't trust them. The prime minister considered that his only hope was the United States, but the Americans were still sitting on the fence, despite everything that President Roosevelt was doing to get the country into the war on the British side.

As always, domestic politics played the major role in American thinking. The rest of the world could be in flames, vanishing rapidly, but first the Americans had to sort out their petty home affairs.

Churchill knew, too, that if disaster overtook Britain again, as it had done at Dunkirk, even Roosevelt would have to wash his hands of the British and become as isolationist as the rest of his fellow citizens. Without a secure base in Europe – in particular, in the British isles – Roosevelt wouldn't have a chance in hell of convincing the US nation to send troops abroad. Hence the deepening crisis in the Middle East had to be resolved – and resolved soon, if he wanted America to enter the war.

But first, Churchill knew, he had to save Malta.

1941

Up came a spider,
Sat down beside her,
Whipped his old bazooka out
And this is what he said...
                    Dirty ditty, 1941

One

'*MALTA!*'

Adolf Hitler smashed his fist down on the map of the Mediterranean – hard. 'Malta muss unser nachstes Ziel sein, meine Herren! It will be the first of the three steps I propose to eradicate the Mediterranean theatre of war from our calculations and make the decisive breakthrough in Russia.' He raised his eyes and gave his generals that hypnotic look of his about which everyone spoke.

They were all generals who had commanded divisions, corps, even armies in the field; highly decorated officers who had been in the army for years and had been staff trained in the best military academies of the world. Yet they listened to this wartime lance-corporal, who had never commanded even a section during his time in the trenches in the 'old war', as if he were the fount of all military wisdom.

'Once we have dealt with Malta, the English will lack their key base in the

Mediterranean. Then our General Rommel here–' he indicated the bronzed officer with his lips covered in ugly red desert sores, 'will make his Afrika Korps drive to Cairo, push on and link up with our brave soldiers in the Caucasus.' Hitler's eyes blazed fanatically. 'Before the real Russian winter sets in, meine Herren, we will have totally eradicated the danger to our southern flank in that accursed country.'

There was a murmur of hear-hears and Blondi, Hitler's Alsatian bitch, wagged her tail happily, as if the praise was aimed at her. In his excitement, Hitler broke wind and Blondi's tail-wagging changed into a whimper. She fled and crouched in the corner of the operations room. Hitler didn't notice and his generals pretended to do the same, but some of them wrinkled their noses and Rommel, who was unwell again, felt his stomach churn at the awful smell.

Hitler continued with, 'A three-pronged attack is planned. From the air, the sea and by parachute.' He paused for the expected gasp of surprise. It came all right and Goering, as fat as ever, stopped rolling his precious diamond worry beads through his lacquered fingers and snorted, 'By parachute, mein Führer! This is the first I have heard of this, sir.'

Hitler didn't make the nasty comment he

would have preferred to direct at the gross fool of an air marshal, whom he had once designated his successor. It wouldn't have gone down well in front of the assembled generals. Instead he barked, 'Herr General Student – report.'

The hard-faced parachute corps commander with the livid scar on his forehead, which he had gained during the airborne invasion of Holland the previous May, snapped his heels together. 'Mein Führer. We have formed a provisional corps of four divisions, two German and two Italian.'

The other brass frowned at the mention of their allies, the Italians. They told themselves they wouldn't be fighting in Africa today, wasting resources, if the Italians hadn't let them down. But as always they said nothing. The Führer was in charge. In his infinite wisdom he must know what he was about, even with the 'spaghetti-eaters'.

'With the assistance of the Italian Royal Air Force', Student went on in that red-faced, no-nonsense manner of his, 'and naturally our own Luftwaffe—'

'The Luftwaffe will never let you down,' Hermann Goering interjected. But no one listened; no one was taking any notice of 'Fat Hermann' now.

'We hope to drop the parachute corps in two lifts, both of sufficient strength to tackle the Tommies on the island,' Student continued after the interruption, while Goering's fat underlip dropped like that of a sulky child. 'Naturally, as is usually the case with airborne operations, we can expect chaos, and the Tommies will probably have a field day shooting our stout fellows as they drop. So we can expect serious losses.'

Hitler understood and nodded. He continued quickly, for the benefit of the other generals, 'Therefore, it is necessary that we make up for the casualties and reinforce General Student here as quickly as possible with seaborne troops from Sicily. The distance between the two islands, as you know, is short. We should, under normal circumstances, be quick ... But of course, there is the problem – it's always there in such operations – presented by the English Royal Navy.'

There was a murmur of agreement from his generals, and this time the Wehrmacht officers were not merely paying lip service to the Führer's conclusions. This time they were serious. As long as the English had their fleet in the Mediterranean any such airborne invasion was at great risk.

Hitler didn't give them time to pose questions. Instead he turned to the sunburned but sick-looking commander of the Afrika Korps and said, with a fleeting smile (for

Rommel was one of his favourites, unlike some of these haughty arrogant 'Monocle Fritzes', as he called his Prussian generals), 'Rommel?'

The stocky Swabian general forgot his worries and answered in that homely peasant accent of his, 'We shall do our best to support this operation by attacking the English Eighth Army. More, my Afrika Korps will make a special point of taking out their North African coastal harbours. We feel that this will occupy the English Navy in the area and, more importantly, what aircraft they may have.'

Hitler slapped his hands together, startling Blondi so much that she turned on her back and exposed her belly as if to show she knew who was the master and was prepared to surrender to whatever he wanted from her. Admiral Doenitz, bitter-faced and grim, standing on the edge of the brass, told himself he was surprised. The assembled generals didn't do the same. They were a bunch of cowardly 'yes-men' at the best of times. They simply didn't have the guts to stand up to the Führer when he was wrong, which happened often, especially in naval matters.

'Excellent, my dear Rommel,' Hitler exclaimed happily. 'That is exactly what I expected of you and what I want personally.

For–' he lowered his coarse voice, as he always did when he wanted to gain the attention of a small audience: it was an old orator's trick, Doenitz knew that, but it worked with the generals; it always would – 'that is the only imponderable with which we are faced. We shall have no trouble with the English Army. We know the English can't fight. However, their navy can–' he paused significantly – 'as long as their fleet enjoys air cover. Without that, I suspect their admirals will not risk their ships, especially the capital ones.' He raised his voice again, as if he was now prepared to close his briefing. 'So, what is to be done?' He answered his own question. 'This. We must gain air supremacy before we start our attack on Malta. In essence, we must knock out every plane the English have there. That will do two things.' He ticked them off on his stubby peasant's fingers. 'One, leave the air over Malta free for our parachute drop.'

Opposite him Student nodded his agreement.

'Two, ensure that the English fleet does not interfere with the second wave of sea-borne troops.'

The generals stamped their boots on the floor in approval and a contemptuous Doenitz couldn't help thinking they were behaving like a bunch of long-haired university students signifying their approval of some important professor who was the key to their obtaining a degree. 'Toadies, the damned lot of them,' he hissed beneath his breath.

'Now,' the Führer continued with a smile, though as always his eyes did not light up, remaining wary and even suspicious, 'how are we to achieve that aim and perhaps more importantly, stop the English from bringing more planes into the island to replace those we destroy?'

Rommel was quickest off the mark. 'My desert air force will do its utmost, mein Führer,' he said, 'to ensure that no planes are flown by the English from Egypt. At this moment we have control of the air over the desert and as it is, the Tommies need every plane they can find to fight there.'

'Well said, Rommel.' Adolf Hitler beamed at his favourite general and again Doenitz's sallow, lined face glowered. He disliked Rommel especially, though he had barely exchanged a word with the general the British were now calling the 'Desert Fox'. And what fools the British were as well, building up the reputation of this German general who was virtually unknown in his own country; they would regret it, he was sure.

'As for the air and air resupply, mein

Führer,' Goering said with apparent casualness, as if there was really no need for him to emphasise the efficiency of his 'flyboys', 'my chaps will take care of them.'

Hitler was not impressed, that was obvious from the sudden sour look on his pudding face. But he said nothing to the air marshal. Instead he turned to Doenitz, the most junior of the senior officers present at the conference. 'Let us hear from you, Doenitz. What about your U-boats – what can they do to help?'

If he were not such a controlled individual, the skinny admiral would have blushed as everyone's gaze turned in his direction, with the senior generals looking down their noses haughtily at him as if he were something unpleasant that had just appeared from the woodwork. Doenitz took his time, however. He let them stare. It was an old trick, but it worked. Suddenly their haughty looks disappeared as they realised that he was not going to be intimidated by them.

'Mein Führer, as you know,' Doenitz commenced, 'I served in those waters as a humble U-boat captain in the old war until my boat was sunk by the Tommies.'

Hitler nodded. He knew how, after being captured, Doenitz had tried to escape from the English POW camp repeatedly, but had

236

finally been released after faking madness. Sometimes he thought when he looked into Doenitz's hard blue unfathomable eyes that the admiral was really mad.

'Around Malta the waters are relatively shallow and difficult to hide in for a submarine. But in order to ensure that not a single supply ship reaches Malta, a U-boat commander would have to have his craft dangerously close to the Maltese shore.'

Hitler nodded his understanding and, with unusual patience for him, waited for Doenitz to continue, while the generals frowned at the time being wasted by this unimportant U-boat commander.

Doenitz let them wait. Outside there was no sound save the regular stamp of the sentries' jackboots on the gravel paths. He knew that he had to time his outrageous suggestion accurately, putting it across in a manner that would not cause the outbursts it could well occasion. He took a deep breath and continued. 'So if we are to seal off any seaborne resupply of Malta's air defences by ship, my U-Boats would suffer grievous casualties. The enemy destroyers would be able to spot them virtually with the naked eye.'

'And so, Doenitz?' Hitler pushed the issue.

'We should use a front ... let someone else take the brunt of the Tommy attack, while my U-boats slip in and carry out my mission.'

'Someone else ... take the brunt of the Tommy attack ... slip in to carry out the mission...' The generals burst out into excited puzzled chatter – like a bunch of silly housewives, Doenitz couldn't help thinking as he paused and waited for the Führer to intervene.

He did. In his thick guttural accent, he exclaimed, 'Aber, meine Herren ... darf ich bitte um Ruhe bitter!'

The silence was immediate. When the Führer asked for quiet, he got it – at once. 'Now, Doenitz,' he said severely. 'What is that supposed to mean? Who else is to take the brunt of the Tommy attack?' He flashed Doenitz a hard look.

'Why, sir,' Doenitz answered, as if it were the most obvious thing in the world, 'the useless Italian submarine fleet!'

Two

It was now autumn.

In the desert Rommel was steadily pushing the British Eighth Army back and back towards Cairo. Soon, as the bronzed but exhausted Eighth Army complained, the 'Benghazi Sweepstakes' would commence: the British front would suddenly break down under Rommel's flank and frontal attacks and the race for safety would begin yet again.

In the Mediterranean all was chaos. British convoys trying to get through to Malta were subjected to aerial and seaborne attacks as soon as they left the safety of Gibraltar. Protected as these convoys were by large forces of Royal Navy ships, sometimes including battleships and the very precious aircraft carriers, they were nevertheless lucky if they reached the besieged island with a handful of the vital supply ships left.

On the island itself, which would be soon awarded the George Cross by George VI,

239

conditions were horrific. Rations were cut for both soldiers and civilians. In turn, the Germans and then the Italians bombed the crowded island. The whole surface seemed to be disappearing, returning to the white rock upon which the villages and cities were built. Fortunately, the Maltese civilians could shelter most of the time in the island's deep caves, but when they ventured out to the surface at night, their houses had vanished, fires burned everywhere, and they had to stand in line for hours, or so it seemed, to get a pail of rationed water.

It wasn't only water and food which were rationed. Ammunition and war supplies were too. At times the AA guns were limited to six shells for a whole day's defence. Even .303 ammunition meant for the machine guns was rationed. As yet another formation of Savoia bombers flew over the camouflaged *Cossack* unharmed because the guns' crews had orders to conserve their ammunition, Scouse complained, 'Bugger this for a tale ...What d'they expect us to do? Knock 'em out of the sky with a wet fart?'

But no one seemed to pay any attention to the Liverpudlian gunner's desperate complaint. And the enemy planes kept on coming, riding the azure blue skies untouched and in majestic triumph.

All the same, the 'buzzes' still continued

on board the *Cossack*. It was clear, naturally, that she would soon sail. If she didn't, she might well be put to the bottom of the Grand Harbour by the persistent bombing; it was only a matter of time.

Other factors played a role too. Her tanks were filled to the brim with precious oil and, although ammunition and food were in short supply on the besieged island, she had taken on board large quantities of both. As the matelots whispered among themselves when they thought there were no officers about – recently the captain had ordered that anyone spreading false rumours would be 'wheeled up in front of him in double quick time' – 'Why so much grub and ammo, mates? We don't need all that stuff to get us to Gib.'

'Yer,' Scouse had agreed. 'You can't tell me they risk all them ships to bring it to Malta for us to take it back to Gib. Don't stand to reason, mates.'

Wide Boy, who had grown unusually quiet since he had been posted back to the *Cossack*, agreed. It didn't stand to reason. So why were they loading so many supplies, if Gibraltar really was their destination.

It was the same question that Number One asked himself. What was the purpose of taking so many precious supply materials away with them? And it was not just the

Cossack. The two other escorts, which he knew were scheduled to sail with her, were also taking on more supplies than the young officer thought necessary for the short trip to Gibraltar. Indeed, one of them, the *Carnation*, looked decidedly unseaworthy with the load she had taken on board.

He had broached the subject with the captain, but the latter seemed preoccupied and not given to much talk. He said he was 'still looking for a bloody cossack hat. You'd think they'd have at least one somewhere on the ruddy island'. But Number One noted that when the skipper went ashore, which was pretty frequently now, he never took one of the horse-drawn cabs to the shopping streets but walked purposelessly through the afternoon heat to naval HQ, as did several others of the captains, both naval and merchant marine, due to sail with the next convoy to leave Malta. Why, he asked himself. But no answers were forthcoming.

At the end of that week a surprise conference was called at naval headquarters. What was really surprising was that it was called for after dark. Why, no one could explain. The island was just as likely to be raided after dark as it was during daylight hours, especially as the water supply was turned on then and the people came out of their cave shelters in droves to collect their ration.

The captain took Number One with him and they found themselves in the operation room of naval headquarters together with a crowd of familiar faces and a few older and stranger ones, fighting for the specially baked plates of meat pies (really tinned bully beef) and large, strong pink gins. Gin was still plentiful, though Number One did suspect it was of the bathtub variety distilled from God knows what by the islanders.

All the younger officers were naturally curious but, filled with gin and their first decent meal of the week, they concentrated on the usual island chat and gossip, waiting for the unknown officer they had been summoned to hear. In the end it turned out to be an elderly commodore in the Merchant Marine, dressed in shabby, stained tunic with faded gold rings denoting his rank on the sleeves. He also wore, of all things, dark glasses. 'Is he bloody blind or something?' one of the flushed junior officers whispered to Number One, as silence fell over the big, high-ceilinged room. 'It's ruddy pitch black outside.'

But when the elderly commodore in the shabby tunic removed his old-fashioned sunglasses, they could all see from those well-remembered keen blue eyes that this particular officer wasn't blind. 'Christ all-bloody-mighty,' the officer who had just spoken breathed in awe. 'It's his nibs ... *in disguise*. It's old ABC himself!'

Admiral Cunningham, the Commander in Chief of the Mediterranean Fleet, looked around his young officers somewhat grimly; then he forced a smile, though over the past few days he had never felt less like smiling. He said, 'Sorry for the theatricals, gentlemen. Don't think the old gent's going off his head. But the Eyeties have more than enough spies on this island. So for the few hours I shall spend in Malta briefing you, you will refer to me as Commodore Jenkins, a retiree of the Merchant Marine brought back to run convoys. Is that clear?'

It was.

Old ABC gave them a craggy smile. 'Furthermore,' he went on, 'what passes in this room in the next hour or so will come under the Official Secrets Act, and I will make sure that anyone who infringes it will be cashiered and sent to prison. I say that not because I am vindictive, but because we are now to embark on a course of action which could influence the whole of the war.' He paused and let his words sink in, noting how the excited young faces became serious and thoughtful and liking the transformation, for it indicated that, boys in uniform as they were, they could be relied on to do their utmost for the old country.

Old ABC clapped his hands and the elegant flunkey at the end of the room solemnly pulled back the black curtain to reveal a large and detailed map of the Mediterranean. They gasped – not because they hadn't seen a map of the Med before, but because the red ribbon marking a shipping route out of the island, presumably for yet another convoy returning to Gibraltar, was definitely an odd shape.

'I see you are surprised,' Old ABC said. 'I understand why. We are all well aware of our usual exit routes for convoys leaving Malta. We keep in shallow water as long as possible, conserving our fuel and at the same time giving those damned Hun U-boats less chance of attacking us because our air cover can easily spot them in shallow water. Then, once we can no longer make use of the shallow water, we go like hell from about here–' he tapped the map with his finger – 'and race for Gib praying for the Sirocco or the Mistral to give us low cloud and air cover. With a bit of luck most of us make it.

'Now, however,' he continued after letting the preliminary information sink in, 'we are going to do something different, as you can see. It won't fool the Huns for long, but I hope it'll work for long enough for us to divert some of the convoy at here – Point X.' Again he tapped the map with the nail of his long crooked forefinger.

The old leather armchairs in which his listeners were seated creaked as they attempted to get a look at 'Point X'. Others gulped down the rest of their pink gins, as if they might be the last drinks they ever swallowed. But all of them were caught by surprise. Old ABC might well have been a dashing destroyer skipper himself as a young man. Now, however, he was an elderly admiral of the fleet – and such high-ranking personages were not given to springing surprises like this, with new convoy routes, Point Xs and even the strange code name for the convoy itself, 'P-10'. What the devil was going on?

Old ABC must have read their thoughts, for he gave one of those strange cackles of his, fully exposing his yellow, ill-fitting false teeth. 'I suppose you fellers think the old man has got a touch of the sun, gone slighty doolally, eh? Perhaps he has. But not today, I can assure you, gentlemen. So what is this business of diverting the convoy at Point X? Why are we trying to fool the Hun with an empty convoy, supposedly on its way to Gib? I shall tell you...'

An hour passed and Old ABC talked solidly all through it, without once referring to notes. Twice the air-raid sirens sounded and enemy planes came in low, machine gunning and dropping 'skip' bombs, while the artillery blasted away at them. Old ABC didn't seem to notice; neither did his listeners, even those of them who had been in Malta too long and were regarded as 'bomb happy'.

The reason was simple. What Old ABC had to tell them was fascinating and made even the humblest 'snotty' there in the darkened operations room realise that he was going to take part in an operation of perhaps war-winning importance.

'So,' Old ABC concluded, 'you see the importance for secrecy till we reach Point X, where each captain involved will receive the usual sealed orders on what he is to do next. But let me end on this.' He looked warningly around his young audience. 'You know, as I told you previously, that the code name for this particular convoy is "P-I0". I realise that it is a strange code name for such an apparently routine convoy. But now you know that this one isn't going to be so routine.' He paused and let his words sink in, while outside the sirens began to sound their dread warning yet again. The braided flunkey in his immaculate whites began to look worried, whether for his own safety or that of his chief, Number One didn't know or care. His mind was racing electrically. He knew now that he was involved in a matter of the greatest importance for the old country, indeed the whole of the British Empire. Would Old ABC's final explanation give him a clue to just what degree of importance was involved for him and the *Cossack* and those other ships which he knew had been selected?

'So what does "P-10" signify?' Old ABC answered his own question. 'Phoenix on the Tenth.'

If Old ABC had expected some noisy outburst at his revelation he was disappointed. Most of his listeners were frankly confused and puzzled by it until, finally, as the drone of the enemy bombers grew ever louder, the old admiral snorted, 'I can see they didn't give you lot much of a classical education at Dartmouth – different in my day. Phoenix! The bloody dicky bird that rises to new life from the bloody flames and ashes! Got it, damn you?'

With that, the aides were hustling their chief swiftly out of the door back to where he had come from, while the first bombs started to whistle down, leaving his audience suddenly standing on their feet at attention, a look of even greater confusion on their faces.

Three

The mail arrived just before the convoy started to leave the Grand Harbour. It was the first post in a month and the deck hands cheered heartily as the post clerk came charging up whipping his donkey feverishly in order to reach the *Cossack* and the rest before the ships sailed.

Excitedly the sacks were collected, some of them singed and smoking a little from the latest raid, which had concentrated on the docks, as if the enemy knew that they were about to sail. Number One, as excited as the rest, knew they knew it: there were plenty of fascist sympathisers among the Maltese who spied for the Italians.

Hastily the purser took charge and, with his clerks, sorted and distributed the mail. Number One tried to discipline himself, smiling winningly as the men hurried off with their precious letters, clutching them to their chests as if they were beloved infants. Then he ripped open his own. They were disappointing: bills from his tailor in

London, a reminder from the Inland Revenue, and a scented letter from his mother in Bournemouth, which was frankly sickening and at the same time a little sad. After all, she still thought he was her 'little boy' and she his 'mummykins' who missed him 'sorely'. She hoped that he would keep himself 'clean in body and mind', as the war 'seems to have had a general coarsening effect on people'. All the same she was very proud of him and 'thrilled beyond words when you had received your medal – everyone in Bournemouth was talking about it'.

Number One smiled a little wanly. He wondered. In Bournemouth they were most probably talking about the cost of maid-servants and the fact that it was virtually impossible to get 'Camp Coffee' any more. All the same, he was pleased to have the letter from the old dear. It meant that someone at least in Blighty remembered that he was still alive, since Claudine, on whom he had spent a small fortune during his last leave in London, hadn't written since telling him, 'I dearly would love to go to bed with you, darling. But I think we ought to save ourselves for when we're married, don't you, darling?' And 'darling' had foolishly agreed. Now he wondered if he would live long enough to get married. He should have fucked her that first night when she had been tipsy and skittish on expensive black-market champagne and she had let him hold her left breast – even tweak her nipple – on the bed at the Savoy.

As usual there were no letters for Scouse. Behind his back, the matelots of his division joked he didn't receive any mail because 'the scouse git don't know nobody who can bloody well write'. Now he wandered around the other sailors, engrossed in their own post, looking over their shoulders enviously and snarling 'gie's a bit to read, mate' or 'is she gonna let yer have it the next time yer on leave?' And he would make an explicit gesture with his forefinger and thumb.

Most of the flushed sailors were too busy to notice. But not Wide Boy. As Scouse leaned over the stanchion near him and peered at the pencilled scrawl and the blurred photo the former was holding, somewhat puzzled, in his right hand, the Liverpudlian asked, 'Who's the kid when he's at home, eh?'

It was a question that Wide Boy found a little difficult to answer, because he had not really been able to decipher the woman's handwriting, which seemed mainly concerned that she had expected an allowance of £1.15.3d, but found she was being paid sixpence less. That aggrieved her. 'I think,' he said hesitantly, 'he belongs to me.'

'What the frig d'yer mean *belongs to me*? Yer mean, it's your nipper?' Momentarily Scouse burst into the ribald ditty frequently sung by drunken matelots. 'Poor little bugger, she's only got one udder to feed the baby on...' The words died on his lips when he saw the sudden look on Wide Boy's face. 'Don't get stroppy,' he said. 'Just thought the nipper don't much look like you. Right pasty, I would have thought. Your bint ain't feeding him proper.'

'Fuck off,' Wide Boy said, unable to think of any other response. Obediently Scouse 'fucked off', swaggering naturally as he did so. Wide Boy told himself that the 'scouse git' would probably swagger to his own funeral, if he could find anyone to bury him. Then he turned his attention to the blurred photo of what he supposed was his son again, with the scrawl on the back stating 'Our Ginger, Age 3 Months'.

What was he to make of it? he asked himself. He was too young to have a child. Besides, he had no future. He had known that since he had been wounded and had broken down after Narvik. All of them, all these happy young sailors, mostly barely out of their teens, were marked by death. They wouldn't survive the war. What value was he to a child? The kid wouldn't even recognise him.

Slowly he started to tear up her – what was her name again? – letter and was about to do the same with the blurred snapshot when the petty officers started to shrill their whistles and the public address system crackled into noisy metallic life. It was the signal to start preparing to leave harbour. Hastily he stuffed the cheap photograph into his pocket and hurried to his duty station as the divisional petty officer started on the usual routine: 'You idle man ... bloody pregnant penguin ... I'll have you on the rattle yet, my lad!...' The war had started for him again.

Four hours later the convoy was just in sight of Malta as the ships plodded on at a steady ten knots westwards, heading – or so it seemed – for Gibraltar. The whole convoy was on red alert, including the merchantmen, and in the leading destroyers, including the battered *Cossack*, they were on double watch, with the officers taking unaccustomed turns about the decks, just as jumpy and nervous as the lookouts. For although the waters hereabouts were shallow and dangerous for enemy submarines, there had still been no sign of their Sunderland flying boat air cover. They would, for the time being, have to rely on the lookouts and the sweating, ashen-faced operators below, crouching over their earphones listening for the first telltale sound of an enemy sub.

Scouse was on watch near the forward Lewis gun. Moodily he crooned one of his own compositions to the tune of 'The Lincolnshire Poacher'. Like most men from his native city, Wide Boy told himself, as he stood his post some ten yards away, Scouse thought himself a wag and something of a singer. Wide Boy had other ideas. Still he listened as Scouse warbled, 'That Hitler's armies can beat us is a lot of cock. Marshal Timoshenko's Red Army boys are pissing through von Bock...' That ended, Scouse was just beginning his own rendition of, 'Tight as a drum, never been done, queen of all the fairies. Isn't it a pity she's only one titty—' when a petty officer snapped, 'Put a sock in it there, man. That voice'd make bloody milk curdle!'

Scouse ceased singing. Under his breath, he started to grumble in that usual surly manner of his, 'Can't a matelot have a bit o' pleasure in this life? I weren't doing no harm—'

Wide Boy interrupted with a sharp, 'Hey, what's that over there?' His voice was suddenly hard and incisive.

'What's what?'

'There, over to port ... That long black—

254

Christ!' Wide Boy hesitated no longer. He clapped both hands around his mouth and yelled desperately at the top of his voice, 'Sir ... *sir* ... Sub off the port bow.' With a practised movement, he swung his chicago piano round and, knowing that it could only be an enemy sub he had spotted there in the shallow water, leased off a frantic burst. The bullets splattered the surface of the water in a furious rain of angry white in the same instant that the alarm bells and klaxons began to sound their urgent, frightening warning. The enemy had been engaged already. Convoy P-10 had commenced fighting for its life.

On the conning tower of U-155, Kapitan-leutnant Dietz, his bearded face hard and set, cocked his head to one side. Yes, there was no mistaking the sound. The Italian submarine which he had been trailing ever since it had sailed from Sicily the previous night with the rest of her squadron had been engaged. He beamed suddenly. The 'Big Lion's' plan was beginning to work. The spaghetti-eaters were going to bear the brunt of the initial engagement. Doenitz's wolf pack would enjoy the fruits of victory.

He bent over the speaking tube and called the engine room. 'Beide Motoren voraus!' he commanded. Almost immediately the U-

155 started to pick up speed, a bone in her teeth. Dietz tugged at his beard thoughtfully. It was still light enough for the Tommies to call upon air support in the form of those long-range Sunderland flying boats of theirs. So he had to be careful. He had to keep his distance from the doomed Italian sub. But at the same time, he had to remain close enough to get a fix on one of the Tommies, slip a tin fish into her and do a bunk before the other escorts came looking for him. But Old Hare, veteran of over a year of undersea warfare – and that was some record – as he was, he told himself he could do it.

Now, as his U-boat gathered speed, Dietz took her down, preparing for an emergency dive just in case. She was running at twelve knots and the cold spray lashed his face time and time again. Still he wiped it away and strained his eyes to catch the first glimpse of the Tommy, ready to press the red 'dive' button immediately. But veteran that he was, he was still anxious. He hated this moment of decision, when one command from him would change relative calm into murder and mayhem; when he could endanger his own life and the lives of his crew by a simple decision and one word – 'ATTACK'. Heaven, arse and cloudburst, no wonder he coughed up his guts every morning that dawn in the captain's own private head... 'I'm living off my shitting nerves,' he told himself and then, as the first red signal flares started to soar into the sky some kilometre or so away, he concentrated on the task on hand.

Ahead of him, the Italian submarine skipper had long thrown doubts and fears overboard. He had been located. Already white tracer was thudding off his submarine's hull, ripping silver holes in the metal, and one radio mast, badly hit, was trailing through the water in his wake. It could be merely a matter of minutes before the English attacked in strength.

'Porco de Madonna!' he cried in anger and despair. 'Avanti ... avanti ... Tenente...'

His flustered young lieutenant, crouched over the gyro-compass and the attack sight below, yelled in turn at the torpedo mates.

Faces lathered in sweat as if rubbed in olive oil, they cried back, 'All lined up ... Ready, sir.'

The young officer called to the captain in the conning tower, bent over the scope, cap turned back to front for easier firing, 'Ready, Captain.'

'Thank you.' The captain forced himself to keep calm and polite. 'Prepare to fire.'

'FIRE!'

There was the sudden hiss of escaping compressed air. The hull shook.

The submarine rose slightly, freed of the torpedoes' weight. The Italian captain pressed his eye tighter to the suction pad of the periscope. Next to him the officer of the watch started to count off the seconds of the running time on his watch. Fascinated, the captain stared through the calibrated glass at the almost stationary British destroyer, he too following the flurry of bubbles which indicated the 'fan' of two torpedoes running just below the surface of the shallow water.

'Uno ... duo...' the officer of the watch intoned, like some sombre priest reading his litany.

To the aft of the destroyer there was a sudden brazen light and a horrid frightening sound like a great piece of canvas being ripped apart. The Italian blinked as the light exploded in front of his eyes. Suddenly, startlingly, the submarine reeled, as if punched by a gigantic fist. Utensils clattered to the deck. Dials burst open. Valves shattered and bulbs popped. There was the sudden shock of rushing water.

Frantically the two officers fumbled for support as the lights flickered off, on and then off again, leaving the interior in pitch darkness. The Italian captain reacted immediately. He pulled himself upright, already feeling the icy seawater beginning to flow around his ankles. 'Emergency lighting!' he cried above the uproar, the screams, shouts and curses of the momentarily panicked crew. As the blood-red lights flickered to illuminate the interior of the sub, the captain gasped.

'Dio mio!' he cried. Water was streaming and spurting through split seams and bulkheads everywhere. His craft was sinking and up above the *Cossack* was preparing to fire another salvo...

At periscope depth, Kapitanleutnant Dietz watched the progress of the tragedy taking place in front of his eyes without feeling. He was not even moved, as most mariners usually were, by the fact that another ship was soon to go to the bottom. He noted the oil slick beginning to spread and the fact that the stern of the Italian sub had now broken the surface at a strange angle, indicating, he knew, that her steering gear had been hit, and told himself that if the Italian skipper didn't surrender in a matter of minutes the Tommies were going to send him and his craft to the bottom of the sea. The English destroyer's aft turret was trained on the Macaroni and at that range not even the buck-teethed Tommies could miss. It was, for the unknown Italian skipper, the moment of truth.

Then it happened, as Dietz had anticipated it would. The destroyer fired. Brazen lights again exploded on the horizon. At that range the English gunners couldn't miss. The first shell struck the submarine's exposed stern with a tremendous hollow boom of steel upon steel. The hull was ripped apart.

'Holy mother of God!' Dietz's second-in-command gasped, crossing himself hastily, while Dietz looked scornfully at such primitive superstition. In the New Germany there was no time for such papist mumbo-jumbo. 'Oh God, help the poor Italian swine.'

But this day God was looking the other way. With a massive loathsome gurgling sound, the Italian submarine, belching oil and compressed air, slid beneath the waves. One moment she was there; the next she was gone, leaving the sea empty of everything save a few pieces of flotsam and a dead man, bobbing up and down gently, drifting away from the scene of the tragedy, as if he might do so for eternity.

Four

Dawn broke, cold, grey and vicious.

A cruel wind tore flatly across the sea. It ripped at the waves with white fingers. Huddled behind bulwarks and boats, the deck hands hid from the flying spray. The wind straight from Africa was so strong that they found it difficult to speak, so they limited themselves to monosyllables, talking only when necessary, the euphoria of the day before, when they had sunk the Italian submarine, vanished.

Still the *Cossack* and her companions ploughed on steadily for Point X, where the skippers in question would open their sealed orders. Food went by the way. Breakfast had been cold, greasy Canadian bacon; lunch would be sandwiches, made with great slimy chunks of bully beef, both washed down with warmish milkless tea, made palatable with a shot of rum.

But no one grumbled, not even that arch-grumbler, Scouse. For all of them sensed this was not an ordinary convoy – their

261

route was different from that taken before – and there was an urgency about it that told them they were on some kind of unusual op.

Number One, watching them like he did usually, a combination of superior officer and guardian angel, thought he had never seen them so dedicated, so absorbed in their duties. So selfless. 'Gawd,' he whispered to himself more than once, 'you'd think the poor sods were in a hurry to go to their own funerals.' For he had a dread sixth sense that Convoy P-10 would end in disaster. He couldn't put his finger on it. It was nothing tangible, just a finger of fear that traced its icy way down the small of his back every now and again.

By the middle of that second day, something did come up which seemed in a way to confirm this sensation of foreboding. The flotilla leader had sighted a sub, just as they started to run out of the shallow water around Malta and felt they had thrown off any potential underwater attacker. As the captain told Number One, 'It's the very bugger. Captain Vian knows he's there. They're getting a distinct ping. There's no mistaking that the ping indicates a sub and not dolphins or any of the usual false alarms. But he simply cannot locate it.'

'A sweep, sir?' Number One suggested.

'They've tried. No luck.'

'Then it can only mean, sir—' Number One commenced.

The captain beat him to it. 'Yes, the U-boat – and I'm sure he's a Jerry, the Eyeties aren't skilled enough to pull off anything like that – is directly underneath one of the convoy.'

Number One whistled softly. He had heard of the dodge before. It was one that took a really skilled U-boat commander – and a very brave one – to carry out. Yet once a German managed to do it, if he navigated his boat skilfully enough, it would take ages to eliminate him. An attack with depth charges, which weren't that selective, would mostly mean the surface craft above the U-boat would be sunk or severely damaged too. All the U-boat skipper had to do was to keep moving at the same pace as the ship above him.

'So what's the drill, sir?' Number One asked after a few moments.

The captain considered. 'Naturally I don't know Captain Vian's thinking on this,' he answered after a few minutes. 'But I imagine he has two alternatives, both rotten.' Again he hesitated, as if he didn't wish to put his thoughts into words.

'Yessir?' Number One urged him.

'The Hun attacks and then tries to make a run for it. Then Vian'll be on to him as quick

263

as a shot.'

'And if he doesn't?'

'Vian waits till he's correctly assessed the U-boat's position, warns the skipper of the boat which is sheltering it–' he shrugged – 'and then goes in regardless of the consequences and knocks both of them, our ship and the enemy one, out of the bloody water.' The captain pushed his cap back and, although it was cold on the bridge, dabbed his brow with his handkerchief, as if he had begun to sweat heavily. 'Either way, that bloody Hun skipper has got us by the frigging short and curlies.'

But Captain Vian had other ideas. He knew he hadn't the time to play a game of cat and mouse with the German U-boat, which had now been located beneath one of the empty freighters. They were within half a day's sailing of Point X and although he didn't know the full details of Old ABC's scheme, he did know just how important it was for the Empire, Malta and the future of the war in the Med. Something had to be done – and done soon. As he told his fellow captains over the radio telephone, 'Gentlemen, I know it's a bloody cliché, but you can't make an omelette without breaking eggs. Therefore, sadly, we might yet be forced to break a few.' The message was cryptic – it was intended to be so in case the

Germans lurking somewhere below them could pick it up. But his captains understood it well enough. Vian was going to act, come what may. He was going to take drastic action.

Thus, while Vian and his little staff pored over their charts and consulted gunnery and torpedo officers in a hectic, hurried attempt to work out a strategy to tackle their unseen opponent, Dietz continued his dogged and daring pursuit of the convoy, right from its midst. He had guessed by now that the Tommies had located him. His operators had reported the sudden flurried activity of many ships' screws above the U-boat when they had first become aware of the enemy among them.

Now that had all settled down to the one steady heartbeat of the freighter some twenty metres above his conning tower, as his navigating officer, the beads of sweat standing out on his furrowed brow in the dim green light, worked to calculate speeds and depths and tried to keep the submarine's position directly beneath their protective shield on the surface.

For his part, Dietz, still relatively unworried and confident, tried to plan how and when he would make a break for it. He knew now that the convoy was well off course if it was sailing for Gibraltar, as

Doenitz had surmised when he had given the wolf pack their orders. It puzzled him. Where in three devils' name were the Tommies going? And why? They were obviously deviating from the usual westwards route for a good reason. After all, another hundred kilometres southwards and they would come within easy range of the Afrika Korps at Derna, Tripoli and the like.

He wondered whether he should stick with the convoy till he found out. But at the same time, if he waited too long he could put himself and his boat in even greater danger, since the Tommies would have better air cover from the landing strips and air bases in Egypt. So he would have to make a break for it and carry out his instructions of torpedoing as many ships as he could by the time darkness fell and his chances of escape from retribution were better. But how and where should he attack?

While the captain of the U-boat was preoccupied with the problems of attack and escape his attention was caught abruptly by the sound of pings on the sound operator's loudspeaker. In an instant everyone ceased doing what he was working at. They froze at their posts, faces pale with shock. Someone was echo-ranging, and they all knew that freighters didn't have echo-ranging equipment. Up above an escort was sending out signals which bounced off the sub's hull. As soon as they were loud enough the escort would know the U-boat's position. 'Verdammte Scheisse!' Dietz cursed to himself. What were the Tommies up to now?

As if rooted to the spot, he and the rest of the crew remained frozen where they were. Suddenly Dietz was overcome by a kind of claustrophobia, the like of which he had never experienced before. It was as if an unseen hand had been shoved beneath the water and was steadily groping its way ever closer to them. And when those unseen fingers grasped the U-boat's hull – what then?

Abruptly, as if he were listening to a stranger, Dietz heard himself order, in a subdued tone, 'Stand by the torpedo tubes!'

The order was cast very softly, but it surprised and relieved the men, even those who were furthest away from the control sector. They breathed a collective sigh of relief. The Old Man had made a decision. And what the Old Man decided was always right. As the torpedo tube doors swung open, the relief on their pale, drawn faces was obvious.

Up above in the *Cossack*, the captain and Number One stared out at the darkening horizon and the rusty old tub of a freighter some five hundred yards or so away on the port bow. She had already half lowered her boats, and those men who were not urgently needed on watch were clustering above them on the deck, clutching their pathetic bits and pieces wrapped in brown paper parcels and bound with ship's twine. A few of them wore helmets, but it was obvious that most of the freighter's crew thought they'd come to no harm, save perhaps being soaked when they had to take to the boats.

'Poor sods,' the captain said to no one in particular, as the helmsman steered the *Cossack* slowly closer to the freighter.

Down on the deck below the on-duty watch viewed the manoeuvre anxiously. They all knew that Captain Vian had given the order to sink the U-boat located somewhere beneath the old tub, and there was nothing they wished for more fervently. Like all destroyer crews they hated the U-boats with a passion. All the same, veterans as most of them were by now, they knew the crew of the freighter would be lucky, damned lucky, if they could escape the bloody clash soon to come.

'Christ Almighty,' Scouse cursed as he stood to with the rest, staring at the doomed freighter, as if they had never seen it before. 'How they gonna do it? A couple of depth charges and the bottom of that rusty old sardine can'll fall right off her. She ain't got a cat's chance in hell.'

Wide Boy felt the same. He had little idea of what tactic Captain Vian had devised to bring the U-boat out of her hiding place beneath the old freighter, but whatever it was it would entail the use of high explosives and, as Scouse had just snorted, the freighter was so old and rusty, hardly a full charge would be needed to blow her apart. He frowned and told himself again that the lot of a matelot at war was hard enough, but that of a merchant seaman was a bloody lot harder. Mostly they didn't have a chance.

The convoy ploughed on.

The steady beat of ship's screws on the surface was getting closer. Dietz found he was beginning to sweat. Cold beads of perspiration started to trickle down the small of his back unpleasantly. He felt himself clenching his fists and tightening his jaw unnecessarily. He ordered himself to stop, only to find himself doing it again a moment later. The screws were very close now. Soon he had to make his final decision. The torpedo tubes were open and the torpedo mates were crouched over their deadly high explosive fish ready to fire at a moment's notice. Still he had to make other provisions. In a low tone, he ordered, 'Rig for depth-charge attack,' and wished fervently he could up periscope and see what was going on on the surface. But he couldn't. He'd have to fight this battle blind.

Two metres away the tubby boat's comedian said in his thick Hamburg accent, 'Thank the Good Lord for what we are about to receive.' He crossed himself with mock solemnity. Nobody laughed.

Now the ship's screws were about two hundred metres away, and for some reason Dietz couldn't fathom the beat seemed to have slowed down somewhat. What were the damned Tommies up to?

Everything was quiet inside the sub. Every piece of machinery had been turned off. The air conditioning which cooled the electrical systems had been switched off, too, and there was no longer a refreshing breeze wafting through the interior. All controls were now adjusted by hand instead of power. Every movement became an effort as the air started to give way. The men sweated freely. The backs of their singlets were black with perspiration. They gasped audibly. But all of this was still unnoticed. For they were all waiting, every man concentrating on what soon must happen and how the Tommies would attempt to winkle them out of their hiding place.

When it came, it did so as a complete

surprise. If they had anticipated a depth charge attack, they were wrong. For the attack came not from above the silent U-boat, but from *below*.

There was a sudden rush. The thrust of compressed air. This was not the click and the clang of a depth charge, but the mighty explosion of a torpedo nearby, its impact striking the submarine's hull like a blow from a gigantic sledgehammer. The next instant the U-155 swung wildly to the right, the lights blinking off, water rushing in from chipped and ruptured plates everywhere. She was out of control, being propelled sidewards at a crazy rate.

'Stand fast ... stand fast, everybody,' Dietz yelled thickly, beginning to cough. The sound was like that of an ancient asthmatic in the throes of a body-wracking fatal attack, for thick acrid yellow fumes were beginning to escape from the ruptured electric batteries which powered the U-boat below the water.

He staggered the best he could, gripping from one hold to another, up the sloping deck to the control section. Here green and red lights were blinking off and on furiously, signalling warnings that his poor dazed head could no longer seem to comprehend. But as the U-boat continued to be propelled sideways as if from a blow of a giant, he could see through blurring eyes that she wasn't sinking. The depth meter was swinging from side to side at a crazy rate. But she wasn't sinking!

'Oil,' he gasped. 'Open the bilge tanks ... oil.' He staggered and nearly collapsed, catching himself just in time. Like figures glimpsed wavering and trembling through a mist, he could just see swaying shapes attempting to carry out the well-rehearsed orders. He gasped his thanks and then the red mist descended upon him and, with his knees giving beneath him like those of a newly born foal, he collapsed and knew no more.

Above on the surface, as the first obscene black bubble exploded like a wet fart and the thick green-grey oil started to spread, the crew of HMS *Cossack* ceased the battle and in bass hoarse unison raised their caps in salute, some of them crying wildly in their exuberance, 'Good old *Cossack*, done it agen,' while on the bridge the captain flung his new fur hat on the deck and jumped on it crazily for some reason known only to himself.

The *Cossack* had done it again!

Five

The wind from Africa had lost its fierceness and it had grown warmer. Over the dark smudge to the south which was the Dark Continent the sun shone faintly and here and there off-duty matelots, trying to escape the fetid overcrowding of below decks were curled under tarpaulins and blankets among the confusion of a wartime destroyer's decks, attempting to sleep.

Those on duty went about their tasks with renewed vigour and happy smiles on their taut faces. The victory of the previous day had cheered them up considerably. The fact that Captain Vian had signalled they should receive a double tot of 'Nelson's Blood' had increased their happiness. Even the fact that half of the convoy, having reached the mysterious Point X, had turned westwards, leaving behind three destroyers to escort three empty merchantmen, had not affected their good mood in any way, though they did remain puzzled, throwing occasional glances to the coast, as if they half expected something – they didn't know what – to appear and explain this mysterious business of 'Convoy P-10'. As Scouse, a little high on 'sippers' he had bullied out of the younger HO men, grumbled, 'It's supposed to be a democracy, ain't it? That's what Churchill keeps telling us, anyhow. You'd think then that them officers'd tell us what's going on. It ain't as if we had any Jerry spies on board.' Angrily he had spat over the side and gone searching for some other teenage newcomer he might be able to bully into giving him a 'sipper'.

As the sun grew higher on the horizon and the little convoy – which, in Wide Boy's opinion, seemed to be circling rather than pushing forward to some British-held African port – slowed down, some of the mystery of Convoy P-10 appeared to be solved. For just about at the time the cooks began serving 'tiddley oggies' – Cornish pasties – and cocoa instead of the normal hot dinner, a fleet of white sails appeared on the horizon, and there was no doubt they were heading straight for the convoy, which had slowed down considerably. Indeed, most of Vian's officers throught privately that they were moving at a very dangerous speed. Any Hun sub spotting them now would make easy meat of them. Yet in their excitement at the appearance of the sailing

274

craft, they conveniently forgot that possibility; they were simply too curious.

Up on the bridge of the *Cossack*, Number One was one of the many destroyer officers watching their approach through his binoculars. He had been able to identify the boats by now. They were the larger size of the Arab dhow, the kind which covered long distances, trading with Southern Africa and as far east as India. He was forced to admire the skill of the Arab skippers, who were making use of every breath of the reduced wind so that their craft seemed to skim across the sparklingly blue sea effortlessly. He could see that the dhows were heading straight for the three empty merchantmen, riding high out of the water with their empty and buoyant holds, as if they already knew their assigments.

Now, as they came ever closer, those who could crowded the railing of the port side to view this curious spectacle, with Vian's yeoman of signals signalling for the second time that no one was to open fire on the strange visitors, Number One could see their decks more clearly.

They were puzzling. For each dhow seemed overly burdened by a large wooden crate out of which something penetrated, painted a kind of yellow camouflaged pattern which he couldn't identify.

'What do you make of 'em?' the captain asked. Despite the growing heat of the day, he was still wearing his cossack hat. He wore it even when he went to 'kip with his old woman', the crew commented.

'Don't know. You mean those crates, sir, I suppose?'

'Yes, I do.' The captain fiddled with his binoculars to improve the focus. 'I'm sure that's what we're here for – to take them on board. But why risk our ships for those? And why the devil all the ruddy secrecy?'

Number One was about to reply, 'Search me, sir,' but then thought the better of it. The Old Man was a bit liverish this morning. Perhaps it was due to the pink gins of the previous night to celebrate the sinking of the U-boat and the DSO which that sinking would now undoubtedly win for him. So he said quietly, 'It's very puzzling, sir.'

It might have been for the two senior officers of the *Cossack*, but not for Captain Vian and his staff officers, who were in the know. They felt a sense of relief that the business of this rendezvous at sea had worked out so well. All the same, they knew they were sitting ducks sailing at this speed and would be making an even better target for any lurking German sub once the freighters stopped to take aboard the precious, top-secret cargo which might well decide the fate of the threatened island of Malta.

Now, as the dhows came close to the freighters and hove to, all was urgent activity. Wide Boy was concentrating on a large crate aboard the nearest dhow, which had been attached to the gantry chain of the nearest freighter and was now dangling awkwardly in mid-air. Slowly he was beginning to make out some of the details of the camouflaged piece. There were large numbers painted on the part he could see, too, though he could not quite make them out nor understand what they signified. But slowly their familiarity eased into his racing mind and he began to identify the item.

Up above him on the bridge, the two *Cossack* officers, equipped as they were with their binoculars, were quicker off the mark. Suddenly, an excited Number One recognised the long piece hanging from the crate, dangling there at the side of the now motionless freighter. 'Holy cow,' he exclaimed. 'Phoenix, old ABC said ... That's what "P" stands for – *Phoenix!*'

The captain flashed a look at him, as if he had suddenly gone mad. 'What the devil are you gabbling about, Number One?' he snapped. 'Touch of the sun or what?'

'No, sir. Now I understand what the C-in-C was waffling about there back in Malta when he mentioned the full name of the op.'

'For God's sake, Number One, draw me a ruddy picture, won't you. I can't understand a damned word of what you're saying!'

But Number One had no time to draw the captain that celebrated picture into which all senior officers invariably wanted to be put. For in the very same instant that he opened his mouth to blurt out the import of his discovery, the klaxons over at Vian's flotilla leader commenced howling faintly and the Aldis lamp behind the bridge started to click off and on, sending its warning signal. The crews on the freighters and the Arabs below in the dhows redoubled their efforts to get the strange cargo stowed and be under way. Suddenly, when everything seemed to be going well, danger was looming on the horizon once again. Malta was not saved yet...

Dietz staggered through the bloody mess of the boat's interior. At least they'd got the fans working again and the U-boat was being flooded with fresh air which was finally driving out the acrid yellow fumes of the damaged batteries. He kicked the bloody severed head of an Obermaat into the scuppers and grasped the tube. 'Up,' he commanded in a voice that he hardly recognised as his own.

The periscope tube squeaked noisily and for one awful moment the wounded U-boat skipper thought the scope wouldn't rise. It did. He peered through the bright calibrated glass as the waves commenced receding. Behind him the gun crew waited for his command to take over the deck gun just in case the torpedo tubes wouldn't work when he needed them. For he guessed he'd only get one chance. His boat was too badly damaged and her speed was reduced to a handful of knots. Now he was engaged in a suicide mission and he knew it. But it didn't matter. If he was going to snuff it, he'd take one of the damned Tommies with him.

The scope cleared. He turned on the enhancer. Everything cleared even more. He saw it was a scene that every U-boat skipper dreamed about. The English freighters had hoved to, with three destroyers circling them like anxious sheepdogs, spread over an area of less than three kilometres. Even with the U-boat in its present sorry state, he knew he couldn't miss.

Suddenly he felt faint. He clutched at the tube hastily. Just in time. Another moment and he would have fallen flat on his face to the wet, littered deck. The wave of nausea swept through him and then it was gone and he felt something like his old self once more. But the surviving crew had seen him stagger and looked worried. He knew why. All their fates depended upon what course of action he took next. Should he flee while he still had a chance, head for Bardia or Derna or one of the other ports held by the Afrika Korps? Or should he fight it out, as Admiral Doenitz, the Big Lion, expected his wolf packs to do?

He turned to face the wretched-looking survivors, some slumped apathetically against the bulkheads, others simply staring into space vacantly, as if they had already given up; one or two with their young faces still animated with the fierce spirit and determination of the U-Boat Arm. 'Kameraden,' he said, 'I think one way or another we shall die.' He spoke without pathos, making his point as if it was a simple statement of fact. 'But we ought, I think, to die for something.' He looked around their worn, smudged faces, those of men, he knew, already destined for death. 'We should not throw our lives for nothing – just like that.' He snapped his thumb and finger together and noticed that one or two of the crew still had sufficient nervous energy to be startled. 'Kameraden, we should die for a cause ... and what better cause is there but that of Greater Germany, our folk and our beloved Führer Adolf Hitler...'

Dietz's voice faltered, as if he had abruptly

lost confidence in his own words and the situation was hopeless. But he was wrong. There was a sudden stirring among the survivors: a kind of facial animation which indicated they were beginning to think – and act – once more. Here and there, weary young sailors raised themselves from the hopeless jumble on the deck of instruments, smashed china, sausages and the other salted dried meats which had been suspended overhead along the length of the sub.

'You see,' Dietz began, new hope surging through his emaciated body, 'we can–' But even as he spoke, he could see that he need not urge them any longer. He had won them over. Already, like sleepwalkers or animals roused from a long hibernation, the ratings were staggering through the chaos to their duty stations, sloshing through the ankle-deep water. Up front, the senior torpedo mate, still bleeding from a deep ugly gash across his forehead, growled in his bass waterfront accent, 'Alles klar, Herr Kalo!'

Dietz threw him a grateful smile. 'Alles klar, Obermaat,' he echoed. 'Stand by for a bow fan of three torpedoes.'

'Zu Befehl!'

Now everywhere the men were taking up their battle stations, even the wounded and injured. The fact that their movement had occasioned a new influx of the water through the buckled, twisted plates of the hull didn't seem to worry them. All of them appeared to be concentrated totally on their tasks.

Dietz nodded his approval. 'Up scope,' he commanded again and twisted his battered white cap to the back of his head. He pressed his head against the periscope, which just touched the surface of the waves. Immediately the targets came in view. The destroyers were beginning to gather speed as they commenced their sweep. He nodded his head defiantly. 'Do what you like, you Tommy bastards,' he said to no one in particular, 'but we're not going down without a fight. We'll take some of you with us. There'll be no more shitting China tea for you lot...'

The whole mysterious rendezvous at Point X forgotten now, the destroyers concentrated on finding the submarine. They knew what the unseen German was after – the freighters. They were a dream target for a U-boat skipper. All the same they knew, too, just how cunning the men of Doenitz's wolf packs were. They had had nearly two years now to perfect their techniques. They were adept at making a supposed attack on one ship – a feint – and then catching another one completely by surprise. Without Captain Vian's skill and experience that first U-boat which they believed to have been sunk would have maintained her position beneath the freighter until it had been time for her to strike and slink away unharmed. No wonder the press back home were calling the U-boats the 'grey wolves'. They were like those predatory creatures slinking silently out of their deep forests to surprise and kill.

So they spread out in a wide sweep, the depth charge teams standing behind their drumlike underwater bombs, the gunners in position at every possible weapon from the turret 4.5 inch guns to the smallest Lewis machine gun, with the lookouts and the officers on the bridge sweeping the sea in a 360-degree arc while below the operators were glued to their direction finders and radar screens, sweating in the fetid fug, as they strained every nerve and sense to catch the first sign of that hated underwater killer.

Wide Boy had found that crumpled photo of the baby as he had fumbled in his pocket for a bit of grubby chocolate he had deposited there. He knew he needed the comfort and energy that its sugar would give him. But instead of chocolate, his hand brought out that poor-quality picture with the pencilled scrawl on the back. For a moment he took his gaze off the sea and stared at it, as if he couldn't quite comprehend what it signified.

Suddenly it came to him. That fragile little piece of humanity was part and parcel of him, too. He stared harder, perhaps trying to identify himself in the baby's pudgy features. But he couldn't. The baby was still too undeveloped. Still, it was him in a way, he told himself, and for the first time in his young life he was struck by the wonder of it all. Whatever happened now – and to him – this little baby would carry his inheritance with him till – He didn't know when. But whenever it was, it struck him that it was vitally important that there would be something left. He doubted if the child would know much about him, save whatever his mother could – or would – tell him of that brief sexual encounter on the wall of an air-raid shelter in a Hull backstreet in the blackout. But—

Wide Boy never finished that thought. For in that particular instant, the excited cry rang out from the bow lookout. 'Torpedo ... starboard bow ... TORPEDO!' And then all hell was let loose.

As the helmsman of the *Cossack* threw the wheel over and she heeled in a tremendous wall of white frothy foam, and the first rattled firing commenced from the destroyers, the first torpedo hissed past, trailing a wake of bubbles behind it.

On the bridge Number One groaned in agony. The damned U-boat skipper knew what he was about. If he missed the destroyer, that same torpedo would be heading straight on a collision course with the freighters some half a mile to their immediate rear. The Hun was damned well going to get one victim at least.

A moment later the second torpedo hissed through the foam, seemingly missing the *Cossack* by a hair's breadth. Now all hell was let loose as the destroyers' guns opened up and the *Cossack*'s captain rapped out his course, trying to ignore the two torpedoes which had just missed the ship and were heading towards the alternative target.

Down below on the deck, Wide Boy gasped with surprise and horror. Obviously the skipper had located the U-boat, which would be at periscope depth watching the tin fish surging through the water. Now he was going to try and ram her; and if things went wrong, not only would the German sub go to the bottom of the Med, but the *Cossack* would too. His heart beating like a crazy trip hammer, knowing there was nothing he could do about it, he watched in petrified fascination.

★   ★   ★

Dietz cursed.

The first torpedo had missed not only the destroyer, but also the stationary freighter loading the strange long wooden crates. Now the destroyer they had just missed had changed course and was coming straight for him. In three devils' name, what was he going to do?

Before he could decide there was a loud explosion. It was followed by a teeth-grinding ripping sound. A hull was being torn apart. He flashed a glance through the scope and cursed angrily. The second torpedo had hit home – but it hadn't struck the freighter. Instead one of the dhows had been virtually ripped in half, with the Arab crew – those who had survived the terrible explosion – throwing themselves in the boiling water, which thrashed and writhed as bits of the shattered hull rained down.

It wasn't just the sinking dhow which had caught Dietz's attention, however. It was the crate dangling from the freighter's crane in mid-air with something now recognisable almost slipping out of the confines of the wooden staves of its container. It was the tailpiece of an aeroplane!

In a flash he realised what the Tommies were up to in this remote rendezvous – and their future intentions. They were going to slip in what was probably a squadron of fighters, to judge by the number of crates he could see being hauled in from the dhows directly to Malta. They'd be concealed from the bombing and German air reconnaissance in the deep caves that were everywhere on the embattled island, and when the Italo-German paradrop took place, they'd slaughter the Reich's brave fallschirmjager just as they'd done at Crete that summer. This time, however, not only the enemy infantry would be defending the island from airborne attack, but fighter planes too. Not only would they make short work of the paratroopers, but the slow lumbering para-transports, the 'Auntie Jus', would be easy meat for the English planes.

He had to do something to stop the English. If he didn't, the Führer might well be unable to launch his proposed airborne invasion of Malta. After all, the airborne attack on Crete had cost him so many of his elite troopers that he had sworn he'd never launch another attack of that nature from the air.

'Surface!' the captain yelled, his own voice virtually unrecognisable now. 'Gun crew on deck ... at the double...!' Dietz knew that there was no time now to prepare an accurate torpedo attack. The destroyer was heading straight for him. But if the gun crew could get the quick-firing deck cannon into action, they might well have time to scupper the Tommies' plans.

There was a clatter of heavy nailed sea boots. The gun crew scrambled up the ladder, which dripped with seawater. They swung themselves over the lip of the conning tower. An English machine gun opened up angrily. Slugs whined off the steel. There was a shower of fiery blue sparks. A gunner screamed in absolute agony and lost his hold. He fell. Dietz dodged just in time. The gunner tumbled backwards. His shattered face looked as if someone had thrown a handful of rich red strawberry jam at it. He slammed to the bottom deck, dead before he hit it.

Now the one-sided battle was reaching its crescendo. Dietz knew they were doomed. It didn't seem to matter. His vision was distorted by the blood-red haze of the lust for death and destruction. Shells from the destroyers were left and right of the submarine wallowing in the shallows, hardly seeming to move. Tracer ripped her length time and time again. Rigging fell in a shower of angry blue sparks. The gun crew fired on desperately. At regular intervals a man slumped on the deck like a bundle of wet abandoned rags. Others went screaming over the side in a desperate flurry of arms and legs to disappear beneath the waves. But there were always other bold, brave men who dashed out through the vicious small arms fire to take up the challenge and help man the gun.

Below the surviving torpedo men worked feverishly in the fading green light to free the last two torpedoes, their faces hollowed out to unreal garish skulls. They hammered and twisted, cursing and sweating, their singlets black with blood as they tried to free the tin fish ready for firing. And all the while the *Cossack* came nearer and nearer, a great white bone in her teeth as she maintained her collision course with the sub.

'Everyone out!' Scouse screamed as A turret filled with gas and smoke under the direct hit from the submarine's 88mm cannon, a great jagged silver hole skewered in the steel box's side. He grabbed a man lying on the floor among the smoking debris. 'Come on, you silly bugger ... Didn't you fucking well hear—' The cry died on his lips. His right hand had penetrated deep into the back of the man's skull. It was thick with blood and red gore. He recoiled, his ugly pockmarked red face filled with horror, but forced himself to get his head together. Pushing the last of the surviving gunners in front of him, he staggered through the wreckage to the outside. Next moment the ammunition still in the turret started to explode, tracer zig-zagging through the holes into the sky like a crazy firework display.

Wide Boy was hit. He had felt himself lifted high in the air, arms and legs whirling. Next moment he had slammed to the deck, the wind knocked out of him momentarily. A huge roaring crimson darkness threatened to engulf him. He shook his head – hard. The darkness vanished. Now the *Cossack* was almost on to the sub. He could see the sinking U-boat quite clearly, in every detail, down to the leaking plates from which oil seeped in a kind of black lava.

'Christ Almighty,' he thought he cried – but perhaps it was only a dying whisper – 'the skipper's gonna ram her.'

Next to him, Scouse, who had seemingly appeared from nowhere, crawling for some reason he couldn't quite make out, croaked hoarsely, 'Crap, said the Lord and ten thousand arseholes bent and took the strain.' He coughed thickly and dark red blood dribbled from the corner of his slack mouth. 'For in them days, the word of the Lord was law.' He slumped and would have fallen full length, but Wide Boy managed to catch and hold him.

Now, as the engines roared full out, they knelt there in their own blood like two fighters at the end of their match, determined not to go down for the count.

'On,' the surviving torpedo mate screamed above the clash of battle above his head.

Dietz knew this was his last chance. 'FIRE,' he yelled back, his voice strangely distorted, as if it was coming from far away.

The dying submarine shuddered. There was the customary hiss of escaping compressed air. The submarine lurched again. The second fish had gone. There were no more. For a moment Dietz slumped over the edge of the conning tower among the wreckage, dead and dying men lying all around him. Somehow he knew it would end like this. He wiped the spray from his ashen face, eyes glazed with the final veil of impending death. He tried to raise his binoculars. But he hadn't the strength. He let them fall back to his chest and peered through the ever-growing mist that was forming before him. The destroyer was coming straight at him at a tremendous pace, a black plume of smoke rising steeply from her shattered midships. He turned his attention to the 'tin fish'. It seemed as if his head was being worked by rusty metal springs, and it took an effort of sheer willpower to do so. They were running true to course. 'God ... please God,' he moaned in his dying moment, 'let them strike!' Then he was falling ... falling ... falling ... that tremendous cry of triumph and might roaring blood-red through his dying brain. 'SIEG HEIL ... Heil H—'

Wide Boy tried to let Scouse fall to the deck gently. But he hadn't the strength. He started to crawl to the abandoned chicago piano. His crazed dying mind was full of one idea – to blast away with that gun at the sinking sub. He had to do it. He *had* to!

HMS *Cossack* was now an indescribable mess. Below decks, they were knee deep in sea water. It gurgled noisily through every shattered plate and hole. It was as if the greedy sea was only too eager to claim it. Everywhere there were the vanished crew's possessions – caps, tins of cigarettes, bottles, mops, brooms. There were the dead too. They lay sprawled out extravagantly, limbs fully extended, lolling back and forth in the shallow water. Others had crawled into tight balls, hands clasped to their ears like small children who had tried to drown out some frightening noise. Even the ship's cat was among them, head sliced cleanly off by a piece of flying shrapnel, lying beneath the old leather settee in the shattered wardroom with the broken picture of George VI still hanging askew on the bullet-pocked wall.

Now this ship of the dead was on its final stretch, fighting to the very last, as if manned by ghosts. It could only take minutes now.

Wide Boy was gasping, as if he were running a great race. Time and time again he paused. He shook his head from side to side in an attempt to remove the descending fog of death. When he succeeded he started to crawl again. His thoughts were no longer rational. They seemed a crazy, jumbled kaleidoscope of speedy flashbacks ... his determination back at Pompey not to stay on the *Cossack* like the rest of those HO idiots ... the banger and Scouse with his bloody grudge fight that never took place ... Number One crying out, 'It's all right, lads, the navy's here' ... the girl asking him to stick it in her ... The events ran off before his dying gaze like scenes from a movie newsreel without the commentary. What did it mean? All that effort. Churchill's blood, sweat and toil ... *for what*?

Suddenly, surprisingly, he found himself slumped behind the chicago piano, his vision wavering, flickering on and off like an electric bulb about to go dead. He forced his head to the ring sight. Again the cross-sight seemed to waver and tremble as if it had a life of its own. He blinked several times. His vision became a little clearer.

Through it he saw that hated sight – a German U-boat wallowing in the trough, obviously sinking, but with that black and red flag with its crooked cross still streaming in the wind defiantly. On the top of the shattered conning tower, he could just make out the white blur of a face. Instinctively he knew it had to be that of the Jerry captain who had done so much harm to his beloved *Cossack*.

'Bastard!' he choked.

He curled his finger round the trigger. He could hardly feel the wet metal, he was so weak. But hate drove him on. With the last of his strength, he pressed the trigger. The chicago piano burst into one final burst of hectic, frenetic life. Then the hot blood flooded Wide Boy's throat. He slumped forward over the gun, splattering blood everywhere in the same instant that Kapitanleutnant Dietz's last torpedo slammed into the *Cossack*.

For Johnny

Do not despair,
For Johnny-head-in-air
He sleeps as sound
As Johnny underground

Fetch out no shroud
For Johnny-in-the-cloud
And keep your tears
For him in after years

Better by far
For Johnny-the-bright-star
To keep your head
And see his children fed.

J. Pudney

Epilogue

The details of what happened to HMS *Cossack* after she had been torpedoed on the night of 21 October 1941 are confused. The explosion just forward of the destroyer's bridge blew off her bows and approximately a third of her forward section. The casualties were horrendous – 159 officers and ratings killed outright and many more wounded.

The survivors – less than a hundred men – were picked up by the two other escorts, the *Carnation* and the *Legion*, and some of the survivors, plus men from the *Carnation*, returned to the drifting ship to put out the fires and attempt to restart her engines. For a while it was thought they would be able to keep the gravely damaged destroyer afloat; it was the fervent wish of what was left of her crew. On the 25th a tug was sent from Gibraltar and an attempt was made to tug the *Cossack*, stern first, back to the Rock. For a few hours things went well. Then the weather worsened. The salvage party was taken off and on the 27th, the tow was

297

slipped. The *Cossack* sank shortly afterwards. It was said that some of the *Cossack*'s survivors wept at the sight.

The years passed, but their Lordships did not forget the *Cossack* and the brave tradition that she exemplified. After all, there had been *Cossack*s in the Royal Navy since 1806. It was decided to commission a sixth *Cossack*. This ship, the last to bear the great name, was completed in August 1945. By that time the war in Europe was well over and the Japanese had just surrendered. Mostly the new *Cossack*'s duties were of a peaceful nature, mainly showing the flag in the Far East, but the last of the line did acquit herself well during the Korean War of 1950–1953. In December 1959, she was finally paid off, however, and she was scrapped in 1961.

Today, four decades later, there is no ship of that name serving in the Royal Navy. The great days of the world's once mightiest fleet are over, just as, for better or worse, all the things that Britain once stood for are. But things, ideas and feelings do not just survive in shape and form and on paper. They survive, too, in men's hearts. The proud veterans of the HMS *Cossack* Association, growing fewer as the years go by, naturally, are such men. Their association flag carries the names of the half-forgotten victories they won when they were young men: Narvik ... Norway ... Malta ... Korea ... A few of them still live who remember that day they boarded the *Altmark* and there was the cry:

'Are there any Englishmen down there?'

to which that famous answer came:

'Then come up. THE NAVY'S HERE!'

Will that navy still be there when the call comes again? the veterans might well ask in our own self-centred time. One wonders ... one wonders...

GLOSSARY OF TERMS

Bangers: sausages
Buzz: rumour
Heads: lavatories
HO men: men recruited for the duration of the war – hostilities only
Matelot: sailor
Nelson's Blood: official tot of issue rum
Number One: first officer
Ping: sound made by Asdic submarine detecting gear
Pom-pom of chicago piano: massed anti-aircraft cannon or machine guns
Purser or Pusser: equivalent to the quartermaster in the army
Rattle: on a charge
Sippers: a sip of issue rum
Three-Stripey: long-service sailor indicated by three red stripes on his arm